SAPPHIRA AND THE SLAVE GIRL

BY

WILLA CATHER

Sapphira
and the
Slave Girl

VINTAGE BOOKS
A Division of Random House, New York

Library of Congress Cataloging in Publication
Data
Cather, Willa Sibert, 1873–1947.
    Sapphira and the slave girl.
    Reprint of the ed. published by Knopf, New
York.
    I. Title.
PZ3.C2858Sap8   [PS3505.A87]   813'.5'2
74–20797
ISBN 0–394–71434–2

CONTENTS

Contents

Book 1

SAPPHIRA AND HER HOUSEHOLD

BOOK I

§ I

The Breakfast Table, 1856.

Henry Colbert, the miller, always breakfasted with his wife — beyond that he appeared irregularly at the family table. At noon, the dinner hour, he was often detained down at the mill. His place was set for him; he might come, or he might send one of the mill-hands to bring him a tray from the kitchen. The Mistress was served promptly. She never questioned as to his whereabouts.

On this morning in March 1856, he walked into the dining-room at eight o'clock, — came up from the mill, where he had been stirring about for two hours or more. He wished his wife good-morning, expressed the hope that she had slept well, and took his seat in the high-backed armchair opposite her. His breakfast was brought in by an old, white-haired coloured man in a striped cotton coat. The Mistress drew the coffee from a silver coffee urn which stood on four curved legs. The china was of good quality (as were all the Mistress's things); surprisingly good to find on the table of a country miller in the Virginia backwoods. Neither the miller nor his wife was native here: they had come from a much richer county, east of the Blue Ridge. They were a strange couple to be found on Back Creek, though they had lived here now for more than thirty years.

The miller was a solid, powerful figure of a man, in whom height and weight agreed. His thick black hair was still damp from the washing he had given his face and head before he came up to the house; it stood up straight and bushy because he had run his fingers through it. His face was full, square, and distinctly florid; a heavy coat of tan made it a reddish brown, like an old port. He was clean-shaven, — unusual in a man of his age and station. His excuse was that a miller's beard got powdered with flour-dust, and when the sweat ran down his face this flour got wet and left him with a beard full of dough. His countenance bespoke a man of upright character, straightforward and determined. It was only his eyes that were puzzling; dark and grave, set far back under a square, heavy brow. Those eyes, reflective, almost dreamy, seemed out of keeping with the simple vigour of his face. The long lashes would have been a charm in a woman.

Colbert drove his mill hard, gave it his life, indeed. He was noted for fair dealing, and was trusted in a community to which he had come a stranger. Trusted, but scarcely liked. The people of Back Creek and Timber Ridge and Hayfield never forgot that he was not one of themselves. He was silent and uncommunicative (a trait they didn't like), and his lack of a Southern accent amounted almost to a foreign accent. His grandfather had come over from Flanders. Henry was born in Loudoun County and had grown up in a neighbourhood of English settlers. He spoke the language as they did, spoke it clearly and decidedly. This was not, on Back Creek, a friendly way of talking.

His wife also spoke differently from the Back Creek people; but they admitted that a woman and an heiress had a right to. Her mother had come out from England — a fact she never forgot. How these two came to be living at the Mill Farm is a long story — too long for a breakfast-table story.

The miller drank his first cup of coffee in silence. The old black man stood behind the Mistress's chair.

"You may go, Washington," she said presently. While she drew another cup of coffee from the urn with her very plump white hands, she addressed her husband: "Major Grimwood stopped by yesterday, on his way to Romney. You should have come up to see him."

"I couldn't leave the mill just then. I had customers who had come a long way with their grain," he replied gravely.

"If you had a foreman, as everyone else has, you would have time to be civil to important visitors."

"And neglect my business? Yes, Sapphira, I know all about these foremen. That is how it is done back in Loudoun County. The boss tells the foreman, and the foreman tells the head nigger, and the head nigger passes it on. I am the first miller who has ever made a living in these parts."

"A poor one at that, we must own," said his wife with an indulgent chuckle. "And speaking of niggers, Major Grimwood tells me his wife is in need of a handy girl just now. He knows my servants are well trained, and he would like to have one of them."

"He must know you train your servants for your own use. We don't sell our people. You might ring for some more bacon. I seem to feel hungry this morning."

She rang a little clapper bell. Washington brought the bacon and again took his place behind his mistress's large, cumbersome chair. She had been sitting in a muse while he served. Now, without speaking to him, she put out her plump hand in the direction of the door. The old man scuttled off in his flapping slippers.

"Of course we don't sell our people," she agreed mildly. "Certainly we would never *offer* any for sale. But to oblige friends is a different matter. And you've often said you don't want to stand in anybody's way. To live in Winchester, in a mansion like the Grimwoods' — any darky would jump at the chance."

"We have none to spare, except such as Major Grimwood wouldn't want. I will tell him so."

Mrs. Colbert went on in her bland, considerate voice: "There is my Nancy, now. I could spare her quite well to oblige Mrs. Grimwood, and she could hardly find a better place. It would be a fine opportunity for her."

The miller flushed a deep red up to the roots of his thick hair. His eyes seemed to sink farther back under his heavy brow as he looked directly at his wife. His look seemed to say: *I see through all this, see to the bottom.* She did not meet his glance. She was gazing thoughtfully at the coffee urn.

Her husband pushed back his plate. "Nancy least of all! Her mother is here, and old Jezebel. Her people have been in your family for four generations. You haven't trained Nancy for Mrs. Grimwood. She stays here."

The icy quality, so effective with her servants, came into Mrs. Colbert's voice as she answered him.

"It's nothing to get flustered about, Henry. As you say, her mother and grandmother and great-grandmother were all Dodderidge niggers. So it seems to me I ought to be allowed to arrange Nancy's future. Her mother would approve. She knows that a proper lady's maid can never be trained out here in this rough country."

The miller's frown darkened. "You can't sell her without my name to the deed of sale, and I will never put it there. You never seemed to understand how, when we first moved up here, your troop of niggers was held against us. This isn't a slave-owning neighbourhood. If you sold a good girl like Nancy off to Winchester, people hereabouts would hold it against you. They would say hard things."

Mrs. Colbert's small mouth twisted. She gave her husband an arch, tolerant smile. "They have talked before, and we've survived. They surely talked when black Till bore a yellow child, after two of your brothers had been hanging round here so much. Some fixed it on Jacob, and some on Guy. Perhaps you have a kind of family feeling about Nancy?"

"You know well enough, Sapphira, it was that painter from Baltimore."

"Perhaps. We got the portraits out of him, anyway, and maybe we got a smart yellow girl into the bargain." Mrs. Colbert laughed discreetly, as if the idea amused and rather pleased her. "Till was within her rights, seeing she had to live with old Jeff. I never hectored her about it."

The miller rose and walked toward the door.

"One moment, Henry." As he turned, she beckoned him back. "You don't really mean you will not allow me to dispose of one of my own servants? You signed when Tom and Jake and Ginny and the others went back."

"Yes, because they were going back among their own kin, and to the country they were born in. But I'll never sign for Nancy."

Mrs. Colbert's pale-blue eyes followed her husband as he went out of the door. Her small mouth twisted mockingly. "Then we must find some other way," she said softly to herself.

Presently she rang for old Washington. When he came she said nothing, being lost in thought, but put her hands on the arms of the square, high-backed chair in which she sat. The old man ran to open two doors. Then he drew his mistress's chair away from the table, picked up a cushion on which her feet had been resting, tucked it under his arm, and gravely wheeled the chair, which proved to be on castors, out of the dining-room, down the long hall, and into Mrs. Colbert's bedchamber.

The Mistress had dropsy and was unable to walk. She could still stand erect to receive visitors: her dresses touched the floor and concealed the deformity of her feet and ankles. She was four years older than her husband — and hated it. This dropsical affliction was all the more cruel in that she had been a very active woman, and had managed the farm as zealously as her husband managed his mill.

§ II

At the hour when Sapphira Dodderidge Colbert was leaving the breakfast table in her wheel-chair, a short, stalwart woman in a sunbonnet, wearing a heavy shawl over her freshly ironed calico dress, was crossing the meadows by a little path which led from the highroad to the Mill House. She was a woman of thirty-six or -seven, though she looked older — looked so much like Henry Colbert that it was not hard to guess she was his daughter. The same set of the head, enduring yet determined, the broad, highly coloured face, the fleshy nose, anchored deeply at the nostrils. She had the miller's grave dark eyes, too, set back under a broad forehead.

After crossing the stile at the Mill House, Mrs. Blake took the path leading back to the negro cabins. She must stop to see Aunt Jezebel, the oldest of the Colbert negroes, who had been failing for some time. Mrs. Blake was always called where there was illness. She had skill and experience in nursing; was certainly a better help to the sick than the country doctor, who had never been away to any medical school, but treated his patients from Buchan's Family Medicine book.

On being told that Aunt Jezebel was asleep, Mrs. Blake passed the kitchen (separated from the dwelling by thirty feet or so), and entered the house by the back door which the servants used when they carried hot food from the kitchen to the dining-room in covered metal dishes. As she went down the long carpeted passage toward Mrs. Colbert's bedchamber, she heard her mother's voice in anger — anger with no heat, a cold, sneering contempt.

"Take it down this minute! You know how to do it right. Take it *down*, I told you! Hairpins do no good. Now you've hurt me, stubborn!"

Then came a smacking sound, three times: the wooden back of a hairbrush striking someone's cheek or arm. Mrs. Blake's firm mouth shut closer as she knocked. The same voice asked forbiddingly:

"Who is there?"

"It's only Rachel."

As Mrs. Blake opened the door, her mother spoke coolly to a young girl crouching beside her chair: "You may go now. And see that you come back in a better humour."

The girl flitted by Mrs. Blake without a sound, her face averted and her shoulders drawn together.

Mrs. Colbert in her wheel-chair was sitting at a dressing-table before a gilt mirror, a white combing-cloth about her shoulders. This she threw off as her daughter entered.

"Take a chair, Rachel. You're early." She spoke politely, but she evidently meant "too early."

"Yes, I'm earlier than I calculated. I stopped to see old Jezebel, but she was asleep, so I came right on in."

Mrs. Colbert smiled. She was always amused when people behaved in character. Sooner than disturb a sick negro woman, Rachel had come in to disturb her at her dressing hour, when it was understood she did not welcome visits from anyone. How like Rachel!

For all Mrs. Blake could see, her mother's grey-and-chestnut hair was in perfect order; combed up high from the neck and braided in a flat oval on the crown, with wavy wings coming down on either side of her forehead.

"You might get me a fresh cap out of the upper drawer, Rachel. I hate a frowsy head in the morning. Thank you. I can arrange it." She pinned the small frill of ribbon and starched muslin over the flat oval. "Now," she said affably, "you might turn me a little, so that I can see you."

Her chair was carved walnut, with a cane back and down-curved arms: one of the dining-room chairs, made over for her use by Mr. Whitford, the country carpenter and coffin-maker. He had cushioned it, and set it on a walnut platform with iron castors underneath. Mrs. Blake turned it so that her mother sat in the sunlight and faced the east windows instead of the looking-glass.

"Well, I suppose it is a good thing Jezebel can sleep so much?"

Mrs. Blake shook her head. "Till can't get her to eat anything. She's weaker every day. She'll not last long."

Mrs. Colbert smiled archly at her daughter's solemn face. "She has managed to last a good while: something into ninety years. I shouldn't care to last that long, should you?"

"No," Mrs. Blake admitted.

"Then I don't think we need make long faces. She has been well taken care of in her old age and her last sickness. I mean to go out to see her; perhaps today. Rachel, I have a letter here from Sister Sarah I must read you." Mrs. Colbert took out her glasses from a reticule attached to the arm of her chair. She read the letter from Winchester chiefly to put an end to conversation. She knew her daughter must have heard her correcting Nancy, and therefore would be glum and disapproving. Never having owned any servants herself, Rachel didn't at all know how to deal with them. Rachel had always been difficult, — rebellious toward the fixed ways which satisfied other folk. Mrs. Colbert had been heartily glad to get her married and out of the house at seventeen.

While the letter was being read, Mrs. Blake sat regarding her mother and thought she looked very well for a woman who had been dropsical nearly five years. True, her malady had taken away her colour; she was always pale now, and, in the morning, something puffy under the eyes. But the eyes themselves were clear; a lively greenish blue, with no depth. Her face was pleasant, very attractive to people who were not irked by the slight shade of placid self-esteem. She bore her disablement with courage; seldom referred to it, sat in her crude invalid's chair as if it were a seat of privilege. She could stand on her feet with a good air when visitors came, could walk to the private closet behind her bedroom on the arm of her maid. Her speech, like her handwriting, was more cultivated than was common in this back-country district. Her daughter sometimes felt a kind of false pleasantness in the voice. Yet, she reflected as she listened to the letter, it was scarcely false — it was the only kind of pleasantness her mother had, — not very warm.

As Mrs. Colbert finished reading, Mrs. Blake said heartily: "That is surely a good letter. Aunt Sarah always writes a good letter."

Mrs. Colbert took off her glasses, glancing at her daughter with a mischievous smile. "You are not put out because she makes fun of your Baptists a little?"

"No. She's a right to. I'd never have joined with the Baptists if I could have got to Winchester to our own Church. But a body likes to have some place to worship. And the Baptists are good people."

"So your father thinks. But then he never did mind to forgather with common people. I suppose that goes with a miller's business."

"Yes, the common folks hereabouts have got to have flour and meal, and there's only one mill for them to come to." Mrs. Blake's voice was rather tart. She wished it hadn't been, when her mother said unexpectedly and quite graciously:

"Well, you've surely been a good friend to them, Rachel."

Mrs. Blake bade her mother good-bye and hurried down the passage. At times she had to speak out for the faith that was in her; faith in the

Baptists not so much as a sect (she still read her English Prayer Book every day), but as well-meaning men and women.

Leaving the house by the back way, she saw the laundry door open, and Nancy inside at the ironing-board. She turned from her path and went into the laundry cabin.

"Well, Nancy, how are you getting on?" She habitually spoke to people of Nancy's world with a resolute cheerfulness which she did not always feel.

The yellow girl flashed a delighted smile, showing all her white teeth. "Purty well, mam, purty well. Oh, do set down, Miz' Blake." She pushed a chair with a broken back in front of her ironing-board. Her eyes brightened with eager affection, though the lids were still red from crying.

"Go on with your ironing, child. I won't hinder you. Is that one of Mother's caps?" pointing to a handful of damp lace which lay on the white sheet.

"Yes'm. This is one of her comp'ny ones. I likes to have 'em nice." She shook out the ball of crumpled lace, blew on it, and began to run a tiny iron about in the gathers. "This is a lil' child's iron. I coaxed it of Miss Sadie Garrett. She didn't use it for nothin', an' it's mighty handy fur the caps."

" Yes, I see it is. You're a good ironer, Nancy."

" Thank you, mam."

Mrs. Blake sat watching Nancy's slender, nimble hands, so flexible that one would say there were no hard bones in them at all: they seemed compressible, like a child's. They were just a shade darker than her face. If her cheeks were pale gold, her hands were what Mrs. Blake called " old gold." She was considering Nancy's case as she sat there (the red marks of the hairbrush were still on the girl's right arm), wondering how much she grieved over the way things were going. Nancy had fallen out of favour with her mistress. Everyone knew it, and no one knew why. Self-respecting negroes never complained of harsh treatment. They made a joke of it, and laughed about it among themselves, as the rough mountain boys did about the lickings they got at school. Nancy had not been trained to humility. Until lately Mrs. Colbert had shown her marked favouritism; gave her pretty clothes to set off her pretty face, and liked to have her in attendance when she had guests or drove abroad.

" Well, child, I must be going," Mrs. Blake said presently. She left the laundry and walked about the negro quarters to look at the multitude of green jonquil spears thrusting up in the beds before the cabins. They would soon be in bloom.

" Easter flowers " was her name for them, but the darkies called them " smoke pipes," because the yellow blossoms were attached to the green stalk at exactly the angle which the bowl of their clay pipes made with the stem.

§ III

The Mill House was of a style well known to all Virginians, since it was built on very much the same pattern as Mount Vernon: two storeys, with a steep-pitched roof and dormer windows. It stood long and thin, and a front porch, supported by square frame posts, ran the length of the house. From this porch the broad green lawn sloped down a long way, to a white picket fence where the mill yard began. Its box-hedged walks were shaded by great sugar maples and old locust trees. All was orderly in front; flower-beds, shrubbery, and a lilac arbour trimmed in an arch beneath which a tall man could walk. Behind the house lay another world; a helter-skelter scattering, like a small village.

Some ten yards from the back door of the house was the kitchen, entirely separate from it, according to the manner of that time. The negro cabins were much farther away. The cabins, the laundry, and the big two-storey smokehouse were

all draped with flowering vines, now just coming
into leaf-bud: Virginia creeper, trumpet vine,
Dutchman's pipe, morning-glories. But the south
side of every cabin was planted with the useful
gourd vine, which grew faster than any other
creeper and bore flowers and fruit at the same time.
In summer the big yellow blossoms kept unfolding
every morning, even after the many little gourds
had grown to such a size one wondered how the
vines could bear their weight. The gourds were
left on the vine until after the first frost, then gathered and put to dry. When they were hard, they
were cut into dippers for drinking, and bowls for
holding meal, butter, lard, gravy, or any tidbit
that might be spirited away from the big kitchen
to one of the cabins. Whatever was carried away
in a gourd was not questioned. The gourd vessels
were invisible to good manners.

From Easter on there would be plenty of flowers growing about the cabins, but no grass. The
"back yard" was hard-beaten clay earth, yellow
in the sun, orderly only on Sundays. Throughout
the working week clothes-lines were strung about,
flapping with red calico dresses, men's shirts and
blue overalls. The ground underneath was littered
with old brooms, spades and hoes, and the rag dolls
and home-made toy wagons of the negro children.
Except in a downpour of rain, the children were

always playing there, in company with kittens, puppies, chickens, ducks that waddled up from the millpond, turkey gobblers which terrorized the little darkies and sometimes bit their naked black legs.

When Sapphira Dodderidge Colbert first moved out to Back Creek Valley with her score of slaves, she was not warmly received. In that out-of-the-way, thinly settled district between Winchester and Romney, not a single family had ever owned more than four or five negroes. This was due partly to poverty — the people were very poor. Much of the land was still wild forest, and lumber was so plentiful that it brought no price at all. The settlers who had come over from Pennsylvania did not believe in slavery, and they owned no negroes. Mrs. Colbert had gradually reduced her force of slaves, selling them back into Loudoun County, whither they were glad to return. Her husband had needed ready money to improve the old mill. Here there were no large, rich farms for the blacks to work, as there were in Loudoun County. Many field-hands were not needed.

Sapphira Dodderidge usually acted upon motives which she disclosed to no one. That was her nature. Her friends in her own county could never discover why she had married Henry Colbert. They spoke of her marriage as "a long step down." The Colberts were termed "immigrants," — as were all settlers who did not come from the British Isles. Old Gabriel Colbert, the grandfather, came from somewhere in Flanders. Henry's own father was a plain man, a miller, and he trained his eldest son to that occupation. The three younger sons were birds of a very different feather. They rode with a fast fox-hunting set. Being shrewd judges of horses, they were welcome in every man's stable. They were even (with a shade of contempt and only occasionally) received in good houses; — not the best houses, to be sure. Henry was a plain, hard-working, little-speaking young man who stayed at home and helped his father. With his father he regularly attended a dissenting church supported by small farmers and artisans. He was certainly no match for Captain Dodderidge's daughter.

True, when Sapphira's two younger sisters were already married, she, at the age of twenty-four, was still single. She saved her face, people said, by making it clear that she was bound down by the care of her invalid father. Captain Dodderidge had been seriously hurt while out hunting; in taking a stone wall, his horse had fallen on him. He survived his injury for three years. After his death, when the property was divided, Sapphira announced her engagement to Henry Colbert, who had never gone to her father's house except on matters of business. After the Captain was crippled and ailing, he often sent for young Henry to advise him about selling his grain, to write his business letters, and to keep an eye on the nominal steward. He had great confidence in Henry's judgment.

Sapphira was usually present at their business conferences, and took some part in their discussions about the management of the farm lands and stock. It was she who rode over the estate to see that the master's orders were carried out. She went to the public sales on market days and bought in cattle and horses, of which she was a knowing judge. When the increase of the flocks or the stables was to be sold, she attended to it with Henry's aid. When the increase of the slave cabins was larger than needed for field and house service, she sold off some of the younger negroes. Captain Dodderidge never sold the servants who had been with his family for a long while. After they were past work, they lived on in their old cabins, well provided for.

When Sapphira announced her engagement, the family friends were more astonished than if she had declared her intention of marrying the gardener. They quizzed the negro servants, who declared that Mr. Henry had never been so much as asked into the parlour. They had never " caught " him talking to Miss Sapphy outside her father's room, much less courting her. After all these years the strangeness of this marriage still came up in conversation when old friends got together. Fat Lizzie, the cook, had whispered to the neighbours on Back Creek: " Folks back home says it seem like Missy an' Mr. Henry wasn't scarcely acquainted befo' de weddin', nor very close acquainted evah since. Him bein' kep' so close at de mill," she would add suavely.

Since she did marry Henry, it was not hard to explain why Sapphira had moved away from her native county, where his plain manners, his calling, vague ancestry, even his Lutheran connections, would have made her social position rather awkward. Once removed several days' journey from her old friends, she could go back to visit them without embarrassment. The miller's unbending, somewhat uncouth figure need never appear upon the scene at all.

The bride chose Back Creek for her place of exile because she owned a very considerable property there, willed to her by an uncle who died when she was still a young girl. On this Back Creek estate there was a mill. It had stood there for some generations, since Revolutionary times.

This farm (and a great tract of forest land afterward sold off) had been deeded by Thomas, Lord Fairfax, to a Nathaniel Dodderidge who came out to Virginia with Fairfax in 1747. Fairfax's actual possessions in the colony were immense; something like five million acres of forest and mountain which had never been surveyed, watered by rivers, great and small, which had never been explored except by the Indians and were nameless except for their unpronounceable Indian names. There was discontent in the Virginia Assembly that so large a territory should be held in one grant. When Fairfax established his final residence in the Shenandoah Valley, he quieted this dissatisfaction by deeding off portions of his estate to desirable settlers, laying out towns, and in every way encouraging immigration.

To Nathaniel Dodderidge he deeded a tract of land on Back Creek. Neither Nathaniel nor any of his descendants had ever lived on this land. It was only after the capture of Quebec by young General Wolfe in 1759 that the mountainous country between Winchester and Romney was altogether safe for settlers. Bands of Indians under

French captains had burned and slaughtered as near Back Creek as the Capon River.

When the danger of Indian raids was over, someone (his name was lost) built a water mill where Henry Colbert's mill now stood. All through the Revolutionary War and ever since, a mill on that site had served the needs of the scattered settlers. The Dodderidges had let the Mill Farm to tenants for successive generations. Sapphira's father had never seen the place. But before his death Sapphira herself, attended by a groom, rode up a four days' journey on horseback to look over her inheritance. One morning she arrived at the Back Creek post office, where a spare room was kept for travellers. Sapphira unpacked her saddle-bags and settled herself for a stay of several days. She rode all over the Mill Farm and the timber land; had a friendly interview with the resident miller and told him she could not renew his lease, which had barely a year to run.

Before Sapphira's marriage to Henry Colbert, carpenters were sent out from Winchester to pull down the old mill house (it was scarcely more than a cabin), and to build the comfortable dwelling which now stood there. When the new house was completed, Sapphira's household goods were carted up from Chestnut Hill and settled in it. She and Henry Colbert were married at Christ

Church, in Winchester, and drove directly to the new Mill House on Back Creek, omitting the elaborate festivities which customarily followed a wedding.

Though it was often said that Miss Dodderidge had broken away from her rightful station, she by no means dropped out of the lives of her family or lost touch with her friends. Until her illness came upon her, she made every year a long visit to the sister who lived at Chestnut Hill, the old estate in Loudoun County. Even now she was always driven to Winchester in March, to stay with her sister Sarah until after Easter. There she attended all the services at Christ Church, where Lord Fairfax, the first patron of the Virginia Dodderidges, was buried beneath the chancel. With the help of her brother-in-law and a cane she limped to the family pew, though she was obliged to remain seated throughout the service. She was a comely figure in the congregation, clad in black silk and white fichu. From lack of exercise she had grown somewhat stout, but she wore stays of the severest make and carried her shoulders high. Her serene face and lively, shallow blue eyes smiled at old friends from under a black velvet bonnet, renewed or "freshened" yearly by the town milliner. She had not at all the air of a countrywoman come to town. No Dodderidge who ever sat in that pew showed her blood to better advantage. The miller, of course, did not accompany her. Although he had been married in Christ Church, by an English rector, he had no love for the Church of England.

§ IV

Mrs. Colbert, in her morning jacket and cap, sat before her desk, writing a letter. She wrote with pauses for deliberation, which was unusual. She was not unhandy with the pen. When writing to her sisters she filled pages with small, neat script, having trained herself to " write small." Postage was accounted dear, and when she sent long letters to relatives in England it was an economy to put a great deal upon a sheet. This morning she was composing a letter to a nephew — a letter of invitation. It was meant to be cordial, but not too cordial. When she felt satisfied with it, she folded the sheet and sealed it with a dab of red wax. Envelopes were little in use. She rang the loud-voiced copper bell, always kept in the side pocket of her chair.

Old Washington appeared. " Yes, Missy? "

" I am minded to drive out, Washington. I have ordered the carriage, and Uncle Jeff must have it at the door presently. Find Till and tell her to come and get me ready."

"Yes, mam."

Mrs. Colbert turned her letter face-down upon her desk. Till could read, and the Mistress did not wish her to see to whom the letter was addressed. When the neat black woman came to the door Mrs. Colbert said cheerfully:

"Now, Till, you must dress me to drive abroad."

"Yes, Missy. The black cashmere, I reckon? It's a wonderful nice day outside, Miss Sapphy. It'll do you good."

Till, Nancy's mother, was a black woman of about forty, straight and spare. Her carriage and deportment and speech were those of a well-trained housekeeper. She knew how to stand when receiving orders, how to meet visitors at the front door, how to make them comfortable in the parlour and see to their wants. She had been trained as parlour maid by the English housekeeper whom Sapphira's mother had brought with her from Devon when she came out to Virginia to marry her American cousin. The housekeeper had seen in Till a "likely" girl who could be taught. Since Mrs. Colbert had lost the use of her feet, Till had charge of everything in the house except the kitchen and fat Lizzie, the cook, whom no one but Mrs. Colbert could control.

Till set about dressing her mistress; took off

the morning jacket and slipped a starched white petticoat and a cashmere dress over Mrs. Colbert's head. "Don't raise yourself up, Miss Sapphy. I'll pull everything down when you has to rise."

"Now the feet, I suppose," said Mrs. Colbert with a shrug. She seldom permitted herself to sigh. "Not the silk stockings. I shan't be getting out anywhere. But you can put on the new kid-leather shoes. They hurt me, but I must be getting used to them."

"Now just you wear the cloth slippers and be easy, Miss Sapphy. Let me wear the kid shoes round the house a few days more an' break 'em in for you."

"Hush, Till. You mustn't baby me," her mistress joked, looking wishfully at the cloth slippers which Till was flapping on her two hands like mittens. "Well, put them on me, but this is the last time. You can't do much at breaking in the new pair, for you have small feet. Almost as small as mine used to be." She regarded her feet and ankles with droll contempt while Till drew on the stockings and tied a ribbon garter below each of her wax-white, swollen knees.

"There's Jeff now," Till exclaimed, as she tied the strings of her mistress's second-best bonnet.

She helped her to rise for a moment and pulled down the full skirts. Washington came at call and pushed Mrs. Colbert's chair through the long hall to the front door. Outside stood the coach, freshly washed; it looked very much like the "four-wheeler" public cab of later days. On the box sat a shrivelled-up old negro in a black coat much too big for him, and all that was left of a coachman's hat. A little black boy came running up to hold the horses, while Jeff descended to help his mistress.

Leaning between Jeff and Washington, Mrs. Colbert crossed the porch and stepped down into the carriage. She settled herself on the leather cushions, and Jefferson was about to close the door when she said quite carelessly:

"Jefferson, what have you got on your feet?"

Jeff crouched. He had nothing at all on his feet. They were as bare as on the day he was born. "Ah thought nobody'd see mah fe-e-t on de box, Missy."

"You did? Take me out driving like some mountain trash, would you? Now you get out of my sight and put on that pair of Mr. Henry's boots I gave you. Step!"

Jefferson scuttled off like an old rat. Washington went to help the boy hold the impatient horses.

Till was leaning in at the carriage door, putting a cushion under her mistress's slippers and a rug over her knees.

"Till," said Mrs. Colbert confidentially, "I wish you would tell me why it's so hard to keep leather on a nigger's feet."

"I jest don't know, Miss Sapphy. The last thing I done was to caution that nigger about his boots. When I seen him wrigglin' his old crooked toes yonder in the gravel, I was that shamed!" Till spoke indignantly. She was ashamed. Jeff was her husband, had been these many years, though it was by no will of hers.

Jeff came back, his pants stuffed into a pair of old boots which needed blacking, and hurriedly climbed on to the box.

"Jeff, you drive careful, now!" Till called. Washington and the black boy stepped back from the horses, and the coach rolled down the driveway. The drive led past the mill, and Sampson, the head mill-hand, came out to wave and call: "Pleasant drive to you, Miss Sapphy!"

To the household it was an occasion when the Mistress drove out. In this backwoods country there were few families Mrs. Colbert cared to call upon, and she had no special liking for rough mountain roads. When the wild laurel was in bloom, or the wild honeysuckle (*Rhododendron nudiflorum*), then she often drove up the winding road to Timber Ridge. She knew she looked to advantage when she stopped to pass the time of day with her neighbours through the lowered window of her coach. Very few people, even in Loudoun County, had glass windows in their carriages. Moreover, on the coach door there was a small patch of colour, the Dodderidge crest: her " coat of arms," the Back Creek people called it. The children along the road used to stare wonderingly at that mysterious stamp of superiority.

This morning when Jefferson came to the place where the mill road turned into the highroad, he asked in his cracked treble:

" Which-a-way, Missy? "

She told him to the post office, so he turned west. When he had gone a mile, he slowed his horses to a walk. There was Mrs. Blake's house, standing under four great maple trees, in a neat yard with a white paling fence. Two little girls ran out, calling: " Good morning, Gran'-ma! "

Jefferson stopped the carriage, and Mrs. Colbert asked after their mother.

" Ma ain't at home," said the older child. " She's gone over to Peughtown. Mrs. Thatcher's dreadful sick. They came for Ma in the night, and brought a horse for her."

"So you are all by yourselves? Suppose you get in and take a ride to the post office?"

The children shot quick glances at each other. The younger one, who was only eight, said timidly: "We've got just our old dresses on, Gran'ma."

Her grandmother laughed. "Oh, never mind, this time! Jump in, the horses don't like to stand. Molly's curls are nice, anyhow."

The children climbed into the carriage, delighted at their good luck. Sometimes, when their grandmother was driving of a Sunday morning, she stopped and took them and their mother as far as the Baptist church; but very seldom had they driven out with her by themselves. This was Saturday, and Molly wished that all her schoolmates could be loitering along the road to see them go by. Her real name was Mary, but since she promised to be a pretty girl, her grandmother had taken a fancy to her and called her Molly. It was understood that this name was Mrs. Colbert's special privilege; her mother and her schoolmates called her Mary. Her little sister was the only one who dared to use Grandmother's name for her.

Uncle Jeff drew his horses up before the long, low, white-painted house where the postmistress lived and performed her official duties. The postmistress herself threw an apron over her head and came out to the carriage. She and Mrs. Colbert greeted each other with marked civility. They held very different opinions on one important subject.

Mrs. Colbert drew from her reticule the letter she had written a few hours ago. "I brought this letter up to you myself, Mrs. Bywaters, because it is important, and I hope you will put it into the mailbag yourself."

"Certainly, Mrs. Colbert. Nobody but me ever handles the mail here. The bag goes from my hands into the stage-driver's. I see you've got your little granddaughters along today."

"Yes, Mrs. Bywaters, this is a pleasant day for a drive. I'd heard you had your house new painted. How nice it looks!"

"Thank you. I had trouble enough getting it done, but it's over at last. I had to tear down all my honeysuckle vines and lay them on the ground. I'm hoping they're not much hurt."

"I hope not, indeed. They were a great ornament to your house, especially the coral honeysuckle. Now, Jefferson, we will stop at the store for a minute. Good day to you, Mrs. Bywaters."

The country store stood across the road from the post office. The storekeeper saw the carriage stop, and came out. Mrs. Colbert asked him to bring her a pound of stick candy, half wintergreen and half peppermint. Both little girls tried to look unconscious, but while their grandmother was talking to the storekeeper, Betty pinched Mary softly to express her feelings. The candy was brought out in a brown paper parcel, but it was not given to them until their grandmother let them out at their own gate. They thanked her very prettily for the candy and the drive.

"Jefferson, you may take me down the turnpike, and out to Mrs. Cowper's on the Peughtown road. I want to ask after my carpets."

As she drove along, Mrs. Colbert was thinking it was fortunate that for once her daughter had been called to nurse in a prosperous family like the Thatchers, who would see that she was well repaid; if not in money, in hams or bacon or a bolt of good cloth. Usually she was called out to some bare mountain cabin where she got nothing but thanks, and likely as not had to take along milk and eggs and her own sheets for the poor creature who was sick. Rachel was poor, and it was not much use to give her things. Whatever she had she took where it was needed most; and Mrs. Colbert certainly didn't intend to keep the whole mountain.

After a few miles of jolting over a rough by-road, she stopped for a call on Mrs. Cowper, the carpet-weaver. At the Mill House all worn-out garments, discarded table linen, and old sheets were cut into narrow strips, sewn together, and wound into fat balls. This was the darkies' regular evening work in winter. When a great many balls of these " carpet-rags " had accumulated, they were sent, with hanks of cotton chain, to Mrs. Cowper, who dyed them with logwood, copperas, or cochineal, then wove them into stout carpets, striped or plain.

§ V

As soon as the Mistress had left the house, Till and her daughter Nancy fell to and began to give her bedroom a thorough cleaning; pushed the bed out from the wall, and washed the closet floors. All the windows were opened, and the rugs before the wash-basin stand and the dressing-table were carried into the back yard and beaten.

After Nancy had pinned a clean antimacassar on the back of the wheel-chair and put the Mistress's slippers ready at the foot of it, her mother said they might as well " give the parlour a lick " before the carriage got back.

The two women, their heads tied up in red cotton handkerchiefs, went into the parlour and rolled up the green paper shades, painted with garden scenes and fountains. The sunlight streamed into the room. The parlour was long in shape, not square, with a low ceiling, the brick fireplace in the middle, under a wide mantel shelf. Horsehair chairs and sofas sat about with tidies on their backs and arms. Captain Dodderidge's old mahogany desk filled one corner. Every inch of the floor was covered by a heavy Wilton carpet, figured with pink roses and green leaves. It was somewhat worn, as it had been "brought over" by Sapphira's mother when she first came out to Virginia. Upon this carpet the two brooms went swiftly to work.

The room had an air of settled comfort and stability; visitors sensed that at once. The deep-set windows made one feel the thickness of the walls. A child could climb up into one of those windows and make a playhouse. Every afternoon Mrs. Colbert was brought into the parlour and sat here for several hours before supper. Here she could watch the light of the sinking sun burn on the great cedars that grew along the farther side of the creek, across from the mill. In winter weather, when the snow was falling over the flower garden and the hedges, that long room, with its six windows and its warm hearth, was a pleasant place to be.

With Nancy at one end and Till at the other, the parlour was soon swept. Till never dawdled over her work. The housekeeper at Chestnut Hill had taught her that the shuffling foot was the mark of an inferior race. After the sweeping came the dusting.

"Now, Nancy, run and fetch me a kitchen chair

and a clean soft rag. I want to git at the po'traits, which I didn't have time to do last week." Any other servant on the place would have stepped coolly on one of the fat horsehair chair-bottoms, — if, indeed, she had thought it worth while to dust the pictures at all, now that the Mistress could no longer reach up and run her fingers along the frames.

When the wooden chair was brought, Till mounted and wiped, first the canvases, then their heavy gilt frames. Her daughter stood gazing up at them: Master and Mistress twenty years ago. Mistress in a garnet velvet gown and real lace, wearing her long earrings and a garnet necklace: a vigorous young woman with chestnut hair and a high colour in her cheeks. The Master in a stock and broadcloth coat, his bushy black hair standing up as it often did now, his face broad and ruddy; he had changed very little. Nancy thought these pictures wonderful. She hoped the painter was really her father, as some folks said. Old Jezebel, her great-grandmother, had whispered to her that was why she had straight black hair with no kink in it.

Anyway, Nancy knew Uncle Jeff wasn't her father, though she always called him "Pappy" and treated him with respect. Her mother had no children by Uncle Jeff, and fat Lizzie, the cook, had left Nancy in no doubt as to the reason. When Nancy was a little girl, Lizzie had coaxed her off into the bushes one Sunday to help her pick gooseberries. There she told her how Miss Sapphy had married Till off to Jeff because he was a "capon man." The child was puzzled, and thought this meant that Jeff had come from somewhere up on the Capon River. But Lizzie made the facts quite clear. Miss Sapphy didn't want a lady's maid to be "havin' chillun all over de place,—always a-carryin' or a-nussin' 'em." So she married Till off to Jeff and "made it wuth her while, the niggers reckoned." Till got the light end of the work and the best of everything. And Lizzie didn't believe that talk about the painter man; she told Nancy that one of Mr. Henry's brothers was her real father. From that day Nancy had felt a horror of Lizzie. She tried not to show it, but Lizzie knew, and she got back at the stuck-up piece whenever she had a chance. She set her own daughter, Bluebell, to spy on Till's girl.

Nancy had never asked Till who her father was. She admired her mother and took pride in what she called her mother's "nice ways." The girl had a natural delicacy of feeling. Ugly sights and ugly words sickened her. She had Till's good manners — with something warmer and more alive. But she was not courageous. When the servants were gossiping at their midday dinner in the big kitchen, if she sensed a dirty joke coming, she slipped away from the table and ran off into the garden. If she felt a reprimand coming, she sometimes lied: lied before she had time to think, or to tell herself that she would be found out in the end. She caught at any pretext to keep off blame or punishment for an hour, a minute. She didn't tell falsehoods deliberately, to get something she wanted; it was always to escape from something.

Nancy was startled out of her reflections about her mysterious father by her mother's voice.

"Now, honey, if I was you, I'd make a nice egg-nog when you hear the carriage comin', an' I'd carry it in to the Mistress when she's got out of the coach an' into her room. I'd take it to her on the small silvah salvah, with a white napkin and some cold biscuit."

Nancy caught her breath, and looked downcast. "Lizzie, she don't like to have me meddlin' round the kitchen to do anything."

"I'll be out around the kitchen, an' Lizzie dassent say anything to *me*. An' if I was you, I wouldn't carry a tray to Missus with no haing-dawg look. I'd smile, an' look happy to serve her, an' she'll smile back."

Nancy shook her head. Her slender hands

dropped limp at her side. "No she won't, Mudder," very low.

"Yes she will, if you smile right, an' don't go shiverin' like a drownded kitten. In all Loudoun County Miss Sapphy was knowed for her good mannahs, an' that she knowed how to treat all folks in their degree."

The daughter hesitated, but did not answer. For nearly a year now she had seemed to have no degree, and her mistress had treated her like an untrustworthy stranger. Before that, ever since she could remember, Miss Sapphy had been very kind to her, had liked her and had shown it. As they were leaving the parlour, Nancy murmured, more to herself than to her mother:

"I knows that fat Lizzie's at the bottom of it, somehow. She's always got a pick on me."

§ VI

The mill stood on the west bank of Back Creek: the big water-wheel hung almost over the stream itself. The creek ran noisily along over a rough stone bottom which here and there churned the dark water into foam. For the most part it was wide and shallow, though there were deep holes between the ledges. The dam, lying in the green meadows above the mill, was fed by springs, and a race conveyed the water to the big wooden wheel.

In the second storey of the mill flour and unground grain were stored; there it was safe in times of high water. The "miller's room," on the first floor, was a recognized feature of every mill in those days; the man in charge slept there and kept an eye on the property, even when no grinding was going on at night. Henry Colbert had no foreman. He himself occupied the room, using it both as sleeping-chamber and office. Years ago he spent the night at the mill only in times of night grinding or high water. But latterly the

mill room had become more and more the place
where he actually lived.

The mill room was all that was left of the
original building which stood there in Revolutionary times. The old chimney was still sound, and
the miller used the slate-paved fireplace in cold
weather. The floor was bare; old boards, very
wide, ax-hewn from great trees before the day of
sawmills. There was no ceiling but the floor of the
storeroom above, with its heavy, ax-dressed cross-
beams. This wooden ceiling, its beams, and the
wooden walls of the room were freshly whitewashed every spring. The miller's furniture was
whitewashed, so to speak, day by day, by the
flour-dust which sifted down from overhead,
and through every crack and crevice in the doors
and walls. Each morning Till's Nancy swept and
dusted the flour away.

Here the miller had arranged everything to his
own liking. The square windows were furnished
with paper blinds, to keep out the four-o'clock
summer dawn if he had been up late the night before. His narrow bed had been made of chestnut
wood by Mr. Whitford, the neighbourhood carpenter and cabinet-maker, and it was a good piece
of work. Bed-cords, hitched about neat knobs,
took the place of springs. On the tightly drawn
cords lay the mattress; a feather " tick " in winter,

a corn-shuck one in summer. His "secretary" was also of chestnut. (Whitford liked to work in that wood.) It was both writing-desk and bookcase. Above the desk four shelves held ledgers and account books, — and a curious assortment of other books as well. The high chest of drawers at which the miller shaved stood between the two west windows, looking toward the house, and his small wood-framed looking-glass hung from a nail driven in the plank wall behind. At seven o'clock every morning little Zach ran down from the house with the master's shaving water in a steaming iron teakettle.

When Henry Colbert first took over the mill, his silent unconvivial nature was against him. A miller was expected to be jovial; to produce whisky, or at least applejack, when a man made a small payment on a long account. In time his neighbours found that though the new miller was stingy of speech, he was not tight with his purse-strings.

One rainy March day at about four o'clock in the afternoon (in Virginia one said four o'clock in the "evening") the miller was sitting at his secretary, going through his ledger. His purpose was to check off the names of debtors to whom he would not, under any circumstance, extend further credit. He found so many of these names already checked once, and even twice, that after frowning over his accounts for a long while, he leaned back in his chair and rubbed his chin. When people were so poor, what was a Christian man to do? They were poor because they were lazy and shiftless, — or, at best, bad managers. Well, he couldn't make folks over, he guessed. And they had to eat. While he sat thinking, Sampson, his head mill-hand, appeared at the door, which was often left ajar in the daytime.

"Mr. Henry, little Zach jist run down from de house sayin' de Mistress would like you to come up, if you ain't too busy."

The miller closed his ledger, glad to escape. "Anything amiss, Sampson?"

"No, sah, I don't reckon so. Zach, he said she was waitin' in de parlour."

Colbert changed his old leather jacket for a black coat, brushed the flour-dust off his broad hat, and walked up through the cold spring drizzle which was making the grass green.

He found his wife dressed for the afternoon, with a lace cap on her head and her rings on her fingers, having her tea by the fire. (When she heard him open the front door she poured his cup, smuggling in a good tot of Jamaica rum, since he didn't take cream.) Before he sat down, he took up a plate of toasted biscuit from the hearth and offered it to his wife. He drank his tea in a few swallows, though it was very hot.

"Thank you, Sapphy. That takes the chill out of a body's bones. It does get damp down there at the mill. Could you spare me another cup?"

Munching his biscuit, he watched her pour the tea. When she reached down for a small red cruet, well concealed on the lower deck of the table, he laughed and rubbed his hands together. "That's why it tastes so good! I must try to get up here oftener when you're having your tea. But it's just about this time of day the farmers come in. The good ones are at work all morning, and the poor sticks never get around to anything at all till the day's 'most gone."

"I'm sure the Master would always be very welcome company in the evenings," replied Mrs. Colbert, lifting her eyebrows, whether archly or ironically it would be hard to say.

"Don't you put on with me, Sapphy." He reached down to the hearth for another biscuit. "You're the master here, and I'm the miller. And that's how I like it to be."

His wife looked at him with an indulgent smile, and shook her head. She stirred her tea gently for a few moments in silence. A log fell apart in the fire and shot up tall flames; the miller put the ends together with the tongs. "Henry," she said suddenly, "do you realize it's getting on towards Easter?"

"And you haven't set out yet," he added. "Have you given up going for this year?"

"No, I wouldn't disappoint Sister Sarah. But Jezebel's been so low. I shouldn't like to be away from home when it happened. I thought she would have gone before this."

Colbert glanced up in surprise. "Well, you needn't put yourself out on Jezebel's account. She may hang on till harvest. It seems like life won't let go of her."

"If you feel that way, what's to hinder my going this Friday? Then I would have all Holy Week with Sarah, and if I get no bad news from home I might stay a week longer. Sarah always entertains after Easter, you know, and I would meet my old friends."

"I can see no objection. The roads ought to be good, if this drizzle don't set into a hard rain. While you're in town you might have the carriage painted. It needs it."

"That's a good idea. And this year I think I shall take Nancy along instead of Till. It would smarten her up, to see how people do things in town."

He considered a moment. " Very well, if you leave Till to look after my place down there. Don't try any more Bluebell on me ! "

His wife replied with her most ladylike laugh, a flash of fun in it. " Poor Bluebell ! Is she never to have a chance to learn? Why are you so set against her ? "

" I can't abide her, or anything about her. If there is one nigger on the place I could thrash with my own hands, it's that Bluebell ! "

The Mistress threw up her hands; this time she laughed so heartily that the rings on her fingers glittered. It was a treat to hear her husband break out like this.

" Well, Henry," as she wiped her eyes with a tiny handkerchief, " I will own to you that if it wasn't for Lizzie's feelings, I'd send that lazy girl off the place tomorrow. I'd give her away ! But we've got the only good cook west of Winchester, and so we have to have Bluebell. Lizzie would always be in the sulks, and when a cook is out of temper she can spoil every dish, just by a turn of the hand. We would never sit down to a good dinner again. Besides, your Baptists would miss Lizzie and Bluebell in the hymns. And they are always being sent for to sing at funerals. I like to hear them myself, of a summer night."

The miller rose, put another log on the fire, and,

by way of an attention, righted the clumsy wheel-chair a little. He took his wife's plump hand and patted it. "Thank you for having me up, Sapphy. It's done me good. The mill room gets very damp between seasons, and I forget to have Tap make a fire. You might send for me a little oftener." He turned up his coat-collar and reached for his hat, but his wife interfered.

"Go and get your shawl out of the hall press. Don't go back to the mill and sit in a damp coat. It's folly to expose yourself. You ought to have a fire every day this weather."

He went into the hall and returned with a great shawl of fine Scotch wool. It had once been dark green, but time and weather had put a dull gold cast into it. He folded it three-cornered, so that it covered his coat, and went out into the drizzle. Military men and prosperous townsmen wore overcoats, but farmers and countrymen wore heavy shawls, fastened with a large shawl-pin.

Sapphira sat looking out at the dripping trees and the thick amethyst clouds which hung low over the mill and blurred the tall cedars across the creek. She smiled faintly; it occurred to her that when they were talking about Bluebell, both she and Henry had been thinking all the while about Nancy. How much, she wondered, did each wish to conceal from the other?

Such speculations were mildly amusing for a woman who did not read a great deal, and who had to sit in a chair all day.

She had given little time to reflection in the years when she was having her children and bringing them up. Even after they were married and gone, the management of the place had kept her busy. Every year there was the gardening and planting, butchering time and meat-curing. Summer meant preserving and jelly-making, the drying of cherries and currants and sweet corn and sliced apples for winter. In those days she often rode her mare to Winchester of a Saturday to be there for the Sunday service. It was because she had been so energetic, and such a good manager, that even from an invalid's chair she was still able to keep her servants well in hand.

Book II

NANCY AND TILL

BOOK II

§ I

On Thursday morning two leather coach trunks were brought down from the garret, and Nancy was allowed, for the first time, to pack them, under Till's direction. Besides the trunks, there was a handy Whitford-made wooden box for shoes, as the poor Mistress had to carry so many pairs. The bandboxes were to go inside the carriage.

By eleven o'clock on Friday morning Mrs. Colbert was dressed and bonneted. All the household gathered round the carriage to see her off. Fat Lizzie brought the lunch-box, for light refreshment on the road to Winchester. The miller came up from the mill to lift his wife into the carriage. Nancy, in her Sunday bonnet and shawl, stood by, expecting to sit on the box with Uncle Jeff, but Mrs. Colbert told her she was to ride inside. The

servants called good wishes as Jeff drove off, and
Henry walked beside the coach as far as the mill.
Nancy had cast an appealing glance at her mother
when she learned she was to sit beside the Mistress.
But Till knew the Dodderidge manners; if the girl
was taken as a companion, she would be treated as
such.

After Till had closed the Mistress's room, she
went down to the mill to "straighten up" for
Mr. Henry. She had her own sense of the ap-
propriate, and she thought the miller's room right
for him, in the same way that Captain Dodderidge's saddle room had always been right. She
approved of the polished chestnut bedstead, and
the counterpane in large blue and white squares,
woven by the same Mrs. Cowper who made carpets. The four brass candlesticks, by which the
miller read after dark, were clean and shining;
only a little tallow from last night had dripped
down the stems. The deep chair beside the reading-table was made of bent hickory withes, very
strong and well fitted to the back. Till had wanted
to make cushions for this chair, but the Master
told her cushions were for women. She was glad
to see that Nancy had kept Mr. Henry's copper
pieces bright: she knew he set great store by these.

Between the whitewashed uprights that held
the board walls together, the miller had fitted

wooden shelves. On these he kept sharp and delicate tools, which the mill-hands were on no account allowed to touch, and a row of copper bowls and tankards which had been his grandfather's.

Nancy had been keeping the mill room in order ever since she was twelve years old. There was nothing down there that could be damaged or broken, the Mistress had remarked to Till; yet the work would be training of a sort.

This morning Till examined everything critically; the bed-cords, the sheets and blankets, the hand wash-basin, the drawer with soap and towels for the miller's private use. She couldn't have kept the room better herself, she thought. On her way back to the house Till fell to wondering for the hundredth time why Nancy had fallen out of favour with the Mistress. To be sure, until lately Miss Sapphy had pampered the girl too much; but it wasn't a Dodderidge trait to turn on anybody they had once taken a fancy to. Nancy herself, Till knew, suspected fat Lizzie as the trouble-maker, but she had never said why.

Old Washington could have given Till some hint as to how this change in the Mistress had come about; but Washington was close-mouthed. Long service had taught him that tattling was sure to get a house-man into trouble.

Nearly a year ago, in the month of May, an

unfortunate incident had occurred. The Mistress, sitting at the table after her husband had finished his breakfast and gone to the mill, heard loud voices from the kitchen. The windows and doors were open to let the fresh spring air blow through the house. She recognized fat Lizzie's rolling tones and suspected she was bullying one of the other servants. Washington was standing behind the Mistress's chair. She beckoned him to help her rise, took his arm, and limped painfully to the back door.

This was what she heard (not Lizzie's voice, now, but Nancy's): "You dasn't talk to me that way, Lizzie. I won't bear it! I'll go to the Master."

Then Lizzie, with a big laugh: "Co'se you'll go to Master! Ain't dat jest what I been tellin' you? You think you mighty nigh owns dat mill. Runnin' down all times a-day and night, carryin' bokays to him. Oh, I seen you many a time! pickin' vi'lets an' bleedin'-hearts an' hidin' 'em under your apron. Yiste'day you took him down de chicken livers fur his lunch I fried for Missus! You're sure runnin' de mill room wid a high han', Miss Yaller Gal, an' you'se always down yonder when you'se wanted."

"'Tain't so! I always hurries. I jest stays long enough to dust de flour away dat gits over everything, an' to make his bed cumfa'ble fur him."

"Lawdy, Lawdy! An' you makes his bed cumfa'ble fur him? Ain't dat nice! I speck! Look out you don't do it once too many. Den it ain't so fine, when somethin' begin to show on you, Miss Yaller Face."

Through Lizzie's lewd laughter broke the frantic voice of a young thing bursting into tears.

"I won't stay here to listen to your nasty tongue! An' him de good kind man to every nigger on de place. Shame on you, you bad woman!" Nancy rushed out of the kitchen sobbing, her face buried in her hands. She did not see her mistress standing in the doorway.

That very night Nancy was ordered to bring her straw tick up from Till's cabin and sleep on the floor outside Mrs. Colbert's bedroom door. She had been sleeping there ever since.

Through the summer, lying outside the Mistress's door was not a hardship, — the girl had always slept on the floor. But when the winter came on, drafts blew through the long hall up at the big house, and even when she went to bed with her yarn stockings on and had heavy quilts over her, the cold kept her awake in the long hours before daybreak.

On nights when the miller did not go down to the mill, but slept in the Mistress's room, and she was not supposed to need a servant ready at call, Nancy was sent running across the back yard to Till's cabin, with her tick in her arms and a glad smile on her face. She loved that cabin, and all her mother's ways. Till and old Jeff slept in the "good room" where there was a bedstead. Nancy spread her mattress on the kitchen floor, where she could watch the firelight flicker on the whitewashed walls as the logs burnt down. There she felt snug, like when she was a little girl. And toward morning she could hear all the homelike noises close at hand: Uncle Jeff snoring, the roosters crowing, the barn dogs barking. Her mammy would maybe come and put an extra quilt over her, and then she would drift off to sleep again.

A few days after Nancy had begun to make her bed outside her mistress's door, the miller came to his breakfast one morning with a grim face. He greeted his wife soberly, sat down, and began to eat his ham and eggs in silence. When his second cup of coffee had been put at his place, he said quietly:

"You may go, Washington, until your mistress rings for you."

As soon as they were alone he lifted his eyes and looked across the table at his wife.

"Sapphira, do you know who has been coming down to clean the mill room lately?"

She looked up artlessly from her plate. "I think it was Bluebell. Don't tell me she meddled with your things!"

"Bluebell; the laziest, trashiest wench on the place!"

"She'll learn, Henry. If she doesn't take hold, I'll send Till down to make her step lively."

"She'll do no stepping at all in the mill. If I see her there again, I'll put her out. Nancy is to look after the mill room, as she always has done."

"But Nancy is old enough now to be trained for a parlour maid. If you won't have Bluebell, try one of Martha's girls. Till has all the housekeeping to do now, since I can't get about. She needs Nancy here."

The miller was silent for a moment. His first flush of anger had passed. When he looked up again, he spoke quietly.

"Of course the blacks on this place belong to you, and I have never interfered with your management of them. But I warn you, Sapphira, that I will not have any of the wenches coming down to the mill. I don't mean to break in another girl. Nancy is quiet and quick. She knows how I want things, and she puts them that way. I must ask you to spare her to me for a little while every morning."

Mrs. Colbert laughed lightly. "Oh, certainly, if you feel that way about it. Why take a small matter so seriously? It's of no importance to me who makes my bed," she added with just a shade of scorn.

"Yes, it is. You wouldn't have anybody but Till fix your room. It's not my bed I care about. It's the girl's quiet ways and respectful manner, and that she never stops to gossip with my mill-hands."

He said no more, but went out into the hall and took up his wide-brimmed hat — this morning white with two days' flour-dust.

When Nancy first began to take care of the mill room, she usually went down while the Master was at breakfast. Sometimes she had to go earlier, to take his freshly ironed shirts and underwear and put them in his chest of drawers before he locked it for the day. After a while she fell into the habit of going early, because she got a smile, along with his "Good morning, child." After her mother and Mrs. Blake, there was no one in the world she loved so much as the Master. She had never had a harsh word from him — not many words at any time, to be sure. But his kindly greeting made her happy; that, and the feeling she was of some use to him.

Once, on a spring morning when the yellow Easter flowers (jonquils) were just bursting into bloom, she had gathered a handful on her way to the mill and put them in one of the copper tankards on the shelf. She thought the yellow flowers looked pretty in the copper. The miller had already gone to breakfast. She didn't know whether she ought to leave them there or not; he might not like her taking such a liberty.

The next morning the flowers were still in the tankard. The miller was stropping his razor. He turned round as she came in.

"Good morning, child. I wonder who brought me some smoke-pipes down here?"

Nancy's yellow cheeks blushed pink. "I just happened to see 'em as I was runnin' down, Mr. Henry. I put 'em in water to keep 'em fresh. An' I reckon I forgot 'em."

"Just leave them there. I like to see flowers in that stein. My father used to drink his malt out of it."

After that, when she could do so unobserved, Nancy often stopped to pick a bunch of whatever flowers were coming on, and took them down to the mill under her apron.

The miller was a little disappointed when

Nancy did not tap at his door before he started for the house, but he never suggested that she come earlier, or delayed his departure by one minute. His silver watch was always beside him while he shaved, and when the hand reached five minutes to eight he put on his hat. The Colbert men had a bad reputation where women were concerned. That was why, in spite of her resemblance to the portrait painter from Cuba, Nancy was often counted as one of the Colbert bastards. Some people said Guy Colbert was her father, others put it on Jacob. Although Henry was a true Colbert in nature, he had not behaved like one, and he had never been charged with a bastard.

The miller lived a rather lonely life, indeed. After supper he usually sat for an hour in the parlour with his wife, then went back to the mill and read. The pages of his Bible were worn thin, and the margins sprinkled with cross-references. When he had lit the four candles on his table and settled himself in his hickory chair, he read with his mind as well as his eyes. And he questioned. He met with contradictions, and they troubled him. He found a comforter in John Bunyan, who also had been troubled. Sometimes he had a bad night, and was awake and dressed a long while before little Zach ran down from the house with his kettle of shaving water. Then he used to watch to see the yellow girl come winding along the garden path: so happy she was — free from care, like the flowers and the birds. He had never realized, until Bluebell took her place for two days, how much love and delicate feeling Nancy put into making his bare room as he liked it. Even when she was scarcely more than a child, he had felt her eagerness to please him. As she grew older he came to identify her with Mercy, Christiana's sweet companion. When he read in the second part of his book, he saw Nancy's face and figure plain in Mercy.

§ II

On the evening after Mrs. Colbert's departure for town, Till felt lonely and downcast. All day she had been busy and resolutely cheerful. Now, as the sun was going down behind the hills, she sat on the doorstep of her cabin watching the long twilight come on.

This was the first year she had ever missed the Easter trip to Winchester with her mistress. She was glad Nancy had been chosen, because it seemed to mean that Miss Sapphy's unaccountable harshness toward the girl was melting. But deep in her heart Till felt slighted and left behind. It was always a great treat for her to stay in Judge Halstead's town house, and to help serve at the dinner parties which Mrs. Halstead gave after Easter. The third sister, Mrs. Bushwell, who now owned Chestnut Hill, came to Winchester at that time, bringing her maid and coachman, and from them Till could hear about everything that had happened at home since last Easter; "home" being always Chestnut Hill.

This mill farm on Back Creek had never been home to Till. She liked, as she said to herself, to live among " folks," not among poor farmers and backwoods people. The finer accomplishments she had learned from Mrs. Matchem, those of which she was most proud, had little chance here. Before the Mistress became an invalid, things were better. Then friends from Winchester often came to stay overnight or to spend a week; there was some satisfaction in keeping the brass and silver bright, the stores of bed linen and table linen bleached. In those days Miss Sapphy used to go back to Chestnut Hill almost every summer for a long visit with her sister, and Till went with her.

Sitting there on her doorstep and remembering happier times, Till found herself shivering. She got up and went into the cabin. When she came back, she had a wool-stuffed bed-quilt about her shoulders. On a still twilight in spring and summer, clouds of fleecy mist curled over the low meadow down where the mill dam was. All Till's secret discontent with the Mill Farm she expressed by the quiet statement that it was " damp." Even on a sunny wash-day the sheets were longer drying than they should be. In the fall the hoar frost was heavier here than over at Mrs. Blake's place on the big road. When Till and the Mistress came back from their Easter fortnight in town, and no fires had been lighted in the parlour, they found damp spots on the English wall-paper.

"They've had moisture up here," Miss Sapphy would remark cheerfully. "All the better for the early roses." She would never admit that it was damper here than elsewhere.

But to Till the heavy atmosphere brought a heaviness of heart. She was not, under any circumstances, a gay darky. In early childhood, at Chestnut Hill, she had suffered a frightful shock. One night, lying in her trundle bed, she was watching her mother dress for the servants' New Year's party. She saw her mother's finery catch fire from a candle; saw her, in flames, run screaming out into the winter wind. The poor woman was fatally burned before the men could overtake her and beat out the fire. As for the child, the negroes declared she had been struck dumb and would never speak again. She said not a word when they tried to comfort her, but looked at them with terrified eyes. Mrs. Matchem, the housekeeper, took Till up to the big house and put her into a cot in her own room. There, away from the emotional darkies, she began to sleep naturally again, and was soon a quick-witted, observant little girl, — but a grave and serious one. So was Mrs. Matchem serious. Till was devoted to her; strove to imitate her in speech and manner. Matchem impressed it upon her that there was all the difference in the world between doing things exactly right and doing them somehow-or-other. The little black girl would stand looking up at the tall Devonshire woman, taking these precepts devoutly to heart. To the sly whispers of the under servants that an easier way was just as good, she steeled herself as if the Bad Man himself were whispering in her ear.

After Captain Dodderidge died, and Miss Sapphy married and went out to Back Creek, her sister, Mrs. Bushwell, bought in Chestnut Hill. All Mrs. Bushwell's interest was in the stables; she left the management of the house entirely to Matchem. Till stayed on, working under Matchem until she was fifteen. Then Sapphira Colbert made a trade for her.

One summer, when she drove down to Chestnut Hill for her yearly visit, Mrs. Colbert took with her a young negro who had a great knack with horses. For two winters she had hired him out to the new blacksmith on Back Creek. This smith had come over from Pennsylvania, and his skill was a wonder to that sleepy community. He could not only shoe and doctor horses; he built good carts and wagons. Mrs. Colbert easily convinced her sister that a boy trained under such a smith would be very useful in her stables. She was willing to part with him in exchange for the girl Till, and a hundred dollars to boot. Mrs. Bushwell, surprised by this liberal offer, closed the deal at once. But Matchem looked down her long nose and compressed her lips.

Till was not unhappy at the prospect of travel and new scenes. She set off in the coach, eager and journey-proud. But from the first night of her arrival at the Mill Farm she had felt buried in the deep woods. For years to come she was homesick for Mrs. Matchem and the open, breezy, well-planted country she had left behind her.

When Sapphira married her off to Jefferson, who was so much older, and whose incapacities were well known among the darkies, Till accepted this arrangement with perfect dignity. How much it hurt her pride no one ever knew; perhaps she did not know herself. Perhaps the strongest desire of her life was to be " respectable and well-placed." Mrs. Matchem had taught her to value position. It was the right thing for a parlour maid and lady's maid to be always presentable and trim of figure. None of the heavy work of a big country house was put upon Till. She always wore a black dress and white apron, neat shoes and stockings. Some years after she had moved her belongings from her attic chamber in the big house over to Jeff's cabin, the Cuban painter came along to do the portraits. He was a long while doing them.

Sitting on the doorstep huddled in her quilt, Till heard a mournful sound come from the deep woods across the creek: the first whippoorwill. She sighed. How she hated the call of that bird! Every spring she had to listen to it, coming out of this resigned, unstirring back-country. Another spring, and here she still was, by the mill-pond and the damp meadows.

Up yonder, at the end of a long road winding through the woods, the level line of Timber Ridge rose like a blue wall. When you had crossed the ridge and gone on a ways, you came to the Capon River. Till had been that far, when the Mistress stayed at Capon Springs to take the baths. On beyond that was Romney, where people of some account lived, she had heard. In front of her, across the creek, she could see the wavering slopes of the North Mountain; no roads up there, just a few wheel-tracks through woods that never ended. Cabins, miles apart; corn patches and potato patches; pumpkins, maybe. Till believed the poor white trash up there lived mostly on the squirrels they shot, and the pig or two they fed on acorns. Down here in the valley, along the big road that led to Winchester, there were some sightly farm-houses, certainly, where well-to-do families lived.

When you got as far as Hayfield church, the woods began to open up, and the country looked more human.

But it wasn't until she caught sight of the red brick springhouse over the Town Spring, a little this way out of Winchester, that Till felt she was back in the world again.

How she loved the first glimpse of cobble-paved streets, with no mud on them! You drove into town by Water Street, lined on either side with neat mansard houses built of pale gray limestone; gray, but almost blue, and not dressed so smooth as to take all the life out of the rugged stone. Such genteel houses they were, opening directly on the street, with green window shutters, and brass knockers; a little walled garden and a hydrant behind each house. Water Street seemed to welcome you to town.

After you drove on and passed Christ Church, then you came to where the quality lived; where Judge Halstead lived; where Miss Sapphy and Nancy were this very night. There the houses had porticos with tall columns, and were set in lawns shaded by flowering trees. How often, when Judge Halstead's "mansion" was lit up for a party, Till had stood at the foot of the stairway in the big hall, waiting to show the ladies to the upper chambers and help them take off their wraps. Whenever the manservant heard the crunch of wheels on the driveway and threw open the front door. . . .

Just then Till heard a very different sound, close at hand. Old Jeff came shuffling along in the dusk. He stopped and stood uneasily before the seated figure.

" It's a-gittin' right late, deery," he said in his squeaky voice.

§ III

As his wife was always in Winchester for Holy
Week, the miller customarily took his Easter dinner with his daughter and granddaughters. This
year Easter Sunday fell early (the twenty-third of
March), but it was a bright, sunshiny morning,
and warm for the season. He walked across the
meadow to accompany Mrs. Blake and her little
girls to church. The children told him joyfully
that Mr. Fairhead, the preacher (who was also
their schoolmaster), was coming to dinner. It
would be like a party; for Mr. Fairhead was not
old and dismal like most preachers, and did not
say a long grace while the chicken was getting cold.

The church was a forlorn weather-boarded
building with neither spire nor bell, standing on a
naked hillside where the rains had washed winding
gutters in the gravelly slope. It had once been
painted red, but the boards were now curling from
lack of paint. It looked like an abandoned fac-
tory left to the mercy of the weather. In the basement underneath, the country day school was kept.

The miller and his daughter went up four warped plank steps and entered the church. Once within, they separated. All the men and boys sat on one side of the aisle, the girls and women on the other. The pews were long benches, with backs but no cushions. There was no floor covering of any kind, there were no blinds at the dusty windows. The peaked shingle roof was supported by whitewashed rafters. Up under this roof, over the front door, was the gallery where the coloured people sat. It was a rule among the farmers who owned slaves to send them to church on Sunday.

While Mrs. Blake knelt for a few moments in silent prayer, Mary and Betty sat restlessly trying to peep over the hats and sunbonnets in front of them to catch sight of their dear Mr. Fairhead, who was in the splint-bottom chair behind the pulpit, waiting for his congregation to assemble.

When the scuffling tramp of heavy shoes on the bare floor had ceased, Mr. Fairhead rose and said: " Let us pray." He closed his eyes and began his invocation. In the untempered light which poured through the bare windows he looked a very young man indeed, with rosy cheeks and yellow hair. He had been sent out into the backwoods to teach the country school and to " fill the pulpit," though he had not yet been ordained. During the long summer vacations he lived in

Winchester and read divinity with old Doctor Sollers, coming out to Back Creek on horseback every Saturday to conduct the Sunday service.

After the prayer he gave out the hymn, read it aloud slowly and distinctly, since many of his congregation could not read. When he closed his hymnbook, the congregation rose. Old Andrew Shand, a Scotchman with wiry red hair and chin whiskers, officially led the singing. He struck his tuning-fork on the back of a bench and began: " There is a Land of Pure Delight," at a weary, drawling pace. But the Colbert negroes, and the miller himself, immediately broke away from Shand and carried the tune along. Mr. Fairhead joined in, looking up at the gallery. For him the singing was the living worship of the Sunday services; the negroes in the loft sang those bright promises and dark warnings with such fervent conviction. Fat Lizzie and her daughter, Bluebell, could be heard above them all. Bluebell had a pretty soprano voice, but Lizzie sang high and low with equal ease. The congregation downstairs knew what a " limb " she was, but no one, except Andy Shand, ever complained because she took a high hand with the hymns. The old people who couldn't read could " hear the words " when Lizzie sang. Neither could Lizzie read, but she knew the hymns by heart. Mr. Fairhead often wondered how it was that she sounded the letter " r " clearly when she sang, though she didn't when she talked.

Could wé but stánd where MÓses stóod
    And viéw the lándscape ó'er
Not Jórdan's stréam nor déath's cold flóod
    Would frígt us fróm that shóre.

When Lizzie rolled out the last verse and sat down, the young preacher looked up at the gallery, not with a smile, exactly, but with appreciation. He often felt like thanking her.

As for Andy Shand, he hated Lizzie and all the Colbert negroes. His animosity extended to the Colberts themselves; even about Mrs. Blake he was " none so sure."

After the congregation was dismissed, Mr. Fairhead and the miller walked down the road together, deep in conversation. Mrs. Blake and her girls followed behind. She knew her father enjoyed the company of an educated man like Fairhead; that was why she had asked the preacher to dinner. Their talk, as she listened to it, was plain farmer talk, to be sure; about the early season, and the prospects for wheat and hay. Presently the miller began to ask about the country school and Mr. Fairhead's pupils. There were bright boys among them, the young man insisted, some who rode over to school from as far as Peughtown. There were even boys from the mountain who would do fairly well if they had half a chance. There was Casper Flight — Here Colbert held up his hand.

" Never say Flight to me, Mr. Fairhead. I've ground that man's miserable bit of corn and buckwheat ten years for nothing, and on top of that he hangs around the mill and steals honest men's grist. My Sampson has caught him time and again crawling down from the storeroom at night with a bag in his hand."

" I know all about him, Mr. Colbert. But if you could see how that corn and buckwheat was raised, you wouldn't grudge grinding it for nothing. They've got no horse, and this boy Casper breaks up the ground in their corn patch and buckwheat field himself. He pulls the plough, and his mother follows at the plough handles and holds the share in the earth. Last spring I got Mr. Giffen up on the ridge to lend Casper a horse, to put in his buckwheat. His father came home unexpectedly, knocked the boy down, took the horse out of the plough, and rode up to Capon River to go fishing."

" I'm glad you told me, sir. If there's any good can come out of the Flights, God knows I'd like to help it along. I could give this boy work around the place in busy times, but you know none of those mountain boys will work along with coloured hands."

"Yes, I know." Mr. Fairhead sighed. "It's the one thing they've got to feel important about — that they're white. It's pitiful."

Whenever Colbert had a talk with David Fairhead, he wished he could see more of him. He had several times asked the young man to supper at the Mill House, but he observed that Fairhead was not at ease in Sapphira's company. He was shy and on his guard, and Sapphira had seemed possessed to puzzle him with light ironies. Since he was from Pennsylvania, she considered him an inferior. Yet her manner with inferiors (with the cobbler, the butcher, the weaver, the storekeeper) was irreproachable. When the old broom-pedlar or the wandering tinsmith happened along, they were always given a place at the dinner table, and she knew just how to talk to them. But with Fairhead she took on a mocking condescension, as if she were all the while ridiculing his simplicity. Therefore, Henry figured it out, she did not really regard him as an inferior, but as an equal — of the wrong kind. Fairhead boarded with Mrs. Bywaters, at the post office, and Sapphira knew that he was "Northern" at heart. She laughed and told Henry she could "smell it on him."

Oh, yes, she admitted, he was not an igno-ramus, like the country schoolteachers who had been there before him. She was glad Mary and Betty had a teacher who did not chew tobacco in the schoolroom or speak like the mountain people. He had doubtless been raised a gentleman — of the Pennsylvania kind. But he was a mealy-mouth, say what you would; and if she made him uncom-fortable, it was because he hadn't the wit to come back at her. "How can I talk to a man who blushes every time I poke fun at him, or at any-body else? You'd better give it up, Henry." So the schoolmaster was not invited to the Mill House again.

Book III

OLD JEZEBEL

BOOK III

§ I

On the first day after her return from town
Mrs. Colbert summoned Till and told her she
meant to go out to see Aunt Jezebel this morning.
"I will have a look around the yard first. Send
Nancy in to dress me, and tell Tap to have the
boys here in about an hour."

The "boys" were young negroes whom Tap
called in from the barn or the fields to help him
carry the Mistress. On each side of her chair were
two iron rings; into these the boys thrust dressed
hickory saplings and bore Mrs. Colbert about the
place. Tap was one of the mill-hands, but he
loved to wait on ladies. He was a handsome boy,
and he knew the Mistress thought so. He used to
make his assistants clean up on these occasions.

" Take off dat sweaty ole rag an' put on a clean shirt fo' de Missus."

This morning the sunshine was so bright that the Mistress carried a tiny parasol with a jointed handle. Her bearers took her along the brick walks bordered by clipped boxwood hedges, — which were dark as yew except for the yellow-green tips of new growth. Mrs. Colbert visited all the flower-beds. The lilac arbour was now in bud, the yellow roses would soon be opening. The Mistress sent Tap for her shears and cut off sprays from the mock-orange bushes, which were filling the air with fragrance. With these in her lap she moved on, until she was carried into old Jezebel's cabin and her chair put down beside the bed.

" You know who it is, don't you, Aunt Jezebel ? "

" Co'se I does, Miss Sapphy! Ain't I knowed you since de day you was bawn ? " The old woman turned on her side to see her mistress better.

She had wasted since Sapphira saw her last. As she lay curled up in bed, she looked very like a lean old grey monkey. (She had been a tall, strapping woman.) Her grizzled wool was twisted up in bits of rag. She was toothless, and her black skin had taken on a greyish cast. Jezebel thought she was about ninety-five. She knew she was eighteen when she was captured and sold to a British slaver, but she was not sure how many years passed before she learned English and began to keep account of time.

Mrs. Colbert put the sprays of syringa down on the pillow, close to the old woman's face. "The mock-oranges are out, I thought you'd like to smell them. There's not a man on the place can tend the shrubs like you did.'

"Thank 'ee, mam. I hepped you set out most all de shrubs on dis place, didn' I? Wasn't nothin' when we first come here but dat ole white lilack tree."

"Those were good times, Auntie. I've been house-bound for a long while now, like you."

"Oh, Missy, cain't dem doctors in Winchester do nothin' fur you? What's dey good fur, anyways?" She broke off with a wheeze.

"There now, you mustn't talk, it catches your breath. We must take what comes to us and be resigned."

"Yes'm, I'se resigned," the old woman whispered.

Mrs. Colbert went on soothingly: "When I sit out on the porch on a day like this, and look around, I often think how we used to get up early and rake over the new flower-beds and transplant before it got hot. And you used to run down to the creek and break off alder branches, and we'd stick them all around the plants we'd set out, to keep the sun off. I expect you remember those things, too."

The old negress looked up at her and nodded.

"Now I'm going to read you a Psalm that will hearten us both." Mrs. Colbert took from her reticule her glasses-case and a Prayer Book, but she opened neither as she repeated: "The Lord is my shepherd."

Jezebel watched her intently, her eyes shining bright under eyelids thin as paper.

When the Mistress finished the Psalm, she called for Nancy, who was waiting in the cabin kitchen in case she might be needed.

"Are the boys outside?"

Then she turned again to the bed. "Have you quilts enough, Jezebel? Do they keep you warm?"

"Yes, Missy, the niggahs is mighty good to me. Dey keeps a flatiron to my feet, an' a bag a hot salt undah my knees. Lizzie, she sends Bluebell down to set wid me a lot. Dat he'ps to pass de time. Her an' Bluebell comes and sings to me, too."

"But Till tells me you don't eat anything. You must eat to keep up your strength."

"Don't want nothin', Missy."

"Can't you think of anything that would taste

good to you? Now think a minute, and tell me. Isn't there something?"

The old woman gave a sly chuckle; one paper eyelid winked, and her eyes gave out a flash of grim humour. "No'm, I cain't think of nothin' I could relish, lessen maybe it was a li'l pickaninny's hand."

Nancy, crouching in a corner, broke out with a startled cry and ran to the foot of the bed. "Oh, she's a-wanderin' agin! She wanders turrible now. Don't stay, Missy! She's out of her haid!"

Mrs. Colbert raised her eyes and gave the girl a cold, steady look. "No need for you to be speaking up. I know your granny through and through. She is no more out of her head than I am." She turned back again to the bed, took up Jezebel's cold grey claw, and patted it. "Good-bye till another time, Auntie. Now you must turn over and have a nap."

She beckoned to the four hands standing outside, and they came with their hickory poles and carried her away.

§ II

Jezebel was the only one of the Colbert negroes who had come from Africa. All the others were, as they proudly said, Virginians; born and raised on the Dodderidge place or on the estates of their Loudoun County neighbours. But Jezebel was brought over from Guinea, that gold coast of the slave-traders, in the seventeen-eighties — about twenty years before the importation of slaves became illegal. She was sold to her first master on the deck of a British slaver in the port of Baltimore.

Her native village in Africa lay well inland, some four days' journey from the sea. It was raided and destroyed by a coast tribe which early in the history of the traffic had become slave-hunters for the slavers. That night of fire and slaughter, when she saw her father brained and her four brothers cut down as they fought, old Jezebel now remembered but dimly. It was all over in a few hours; of the village nothing was left but smoking ashes and mutilated bodies. By morning she and her fellow captives were in leg chains and on their march to the sea.

When they reached the coast they were kept in the stockade only long enough to be stripped, shaved all over the body, and drenched with sea water. An English vessel, the *Albert Horn,* lay at anchor out in the gulf, with nearly a full cargo of negroes stowed on board. The wind was good, and the skipper was waiting impatiently for the booty of this last raid.

Jezebel and the other captives were rowed out in small boats and put on board in leg chains; they came from a fierce cannibal people, and had not been broken in by weeks of discipline in the stockade.

When the *Albert Horn* was under sail, and the blue lines of the inland mountains began to grow dim, the fetters were taken off the female captives. They were not likely to make trouble.

The *Albert Horn,* built for the slave trade, had two decks. The negroes were stowed between the upper and lower decks, on a platform as long and as wide as the vessel; but there was only three feet ten inches between the shelf on which they lay and the upper deck which roofed them over. The slaves made the long voyage of from two to three months in a sitting or recumbent position, on a plank floor, with very little space, if any, between their bare bodies. The males were stowed forward of the main hatch, the women aft. All were kept naked throughout the voyage, and their heads and bodies were shaved every fortnight. As there was no drainage of any sort, the slaves' quarters, and the creatures in them, got very foul overnight. Every morning the " 'tween decks " and its inmates were cleaned off with streams of sea water from the hose. The Captain of the *Albert Horn* was not a brutal man, and his vessel was a model slaver. Except in rough weather, the males, ironed two and two, were allowed out on the lower deck for a few hours while their platform was being scrubbed and fumigated. At the same time, the women were turned out on the lower after deck without chains.

On the first night after the *Albert Horn* got under way, the sailors gave Jezebel the name she had borne ever since. When the two hands detailed to watch the after 'tween decks had seen that all the females were lying in the spaces assigned to them, they put out their lanterns and went on deck to take the air. A little later the second mate, hearing shrieks and screams from the women's quarters, ran down from his cabin to find the guards flogging a girl they had dragged out from a heap of rolling, howling blacks.

" It's this here Jezebel made all the row, sir," one of the men panted.

The mate made a dash and drove at her throat to throttle her, but she was too quick for him. She snapped like a mastiff and bit through the ball of his thumb.

Next morning the mate felt an ominous throbbing in his hand. He reported the fracas to the Captain, saying he didn't see anything for it but to throw the female gorilla overboard. She could never be tamed.

The skipper feared his mate might be in for a bad infection; but he had a third interest in the cargo, and he wasn't anxious to throw any of it overboard. He thought he would like to see a girl who could stand up against two men and the cat.

"Clean her off and put a bridle on her, and bring her up," he told the mate. Himself, he never went near the slave deck; he couldn't stand the smell.

Jezebel was brought up in heavy irons for his inspection. Her naked back was seamed with welts and bloody cuts, but she carried herself with proud indifference, and there was no plea for mercy in her eyes. The skipper told the seamen in charge to loosen the noose round her neck. As he walked up and down, smoking his pipe, he looked her well over. He judged this girl was worth any three of the women, — as much as the best of the men. Anatomically she was remarkable, for

an African negress: tall, straight, muscular, long
in the legs. The skipper had a kind of respect for
a well-shaped creature; horse, cow, or woman.
And he respected anybody who could take a flogging like that without buckling.

He gave orders that Jezebel was not to go back
between decks. She was to be kept on the upper
deck in all weathers, fastened with a light chain to
the deck rail. She was to be given a sailor's jacket
to cover her wounds, and at night she was to be
provided with a tarpaulin.

After she was thus isolated, the girl gave no
more trouble, — though she always laughed aloud
when the second mate passed with his arm in a
sling. The voyage was long and rough. Jezebel
was knocked about and drenched by heavy seas,
and was sometimes seasick, but she made no com-
plaint. When the seamen hosed out the scupper,
she took off her jacket and invited the stream of
salt water over her body. Except for a few long
scars on her back and thighs, there was nothing
now to show what had happened the first night
she came on board.

When the *Albert Horn* at last reached Baltimore, her skipper kept her out at anchor until buy-
ers from Maryland and Virginia could be notified
and arrive. Jezebel, he noticed, regarded the
water line of the city with lively curiosity, quite

different from the hopeless indifference on the faces of her fellow captives.

" She'll make the best sale of the lot," he told the mate.

In the first boat-load of purchasers who came out to inspect the skipper's cargo, there was a Dutch dairy farmer. He brought with him the country doctor of his neighbourhood. The dairyman and his friend, the doctor, were in no hurry. They looked over a great number of negroes. To Jezebel they gave a searching physical examination, talking together in the low Dutch vernacular, and asking no questions of the skipper. The dairyman called attention to the whip scars on her body, and beckoned the second mate.

" Disposition? " he asked.

" The niggers who captured her did that. She put up a fight. Strong as an ox."

The Dutchman himself looked very like an ox, but the doctor looked kind and shrewd. He fumbled in his pocket and brought out a deerskin pouch, from which he took two squares of maple sugar. One he put in his own mouth, and smacked his lips. The other he offered to Jezebel with a questioning smile. She opened her jaws. At this the second mate, standing by, looked the other way. The doctor put the sugar on Jezebel's tongue. She crunched it, grinned, and stuck out her tongue for more. The doctor gave his friend the deciding nod. The Dutchman paid the skipper's price, took Jezebel into Baltimore, and stowed her in the heavy wagon in which he had come to town.

When he reached home, he set about breaking in his new wench. On the journey from Baltimore he had discovered that her personal manners were too strong for even a Dutch farmer's household, so he lodged her in the haymow over the cow barn. She learned to milk the cows and to do all the stable work, but she was kept in the barn and was never allowed to touch the butter. The dairy farmer died in an outbreak of smallpox; his widow promptly sold Jezebel. She had been owned by several masters and had learned some English before the Dodderidge farm steward bought her. She went to the Dodderidges the year that Sapphira was born, and had been in the family ever since.

Until Jezebel was eighty years old, Sapphira had entrusted her to oversee the gardens at the Mill Farm. As late as last spring she still got out to sit in the sun and watch the boys who did the shrubbery and shaped the hedges. In wintertime she stayed in her cabin, sewed carpet-rags, and patched the farm-hands' shirts and breeches. She meted out justice by giving a slack boy a rough seat in his breeches, and a likely boy a smooth seat. When Manuel, since dead, had come to her whining that "his pants wasn't comf'able," she gave him a scornful look and said:

"You ain't no call to be comf'able, you settin' down de minute a body's back's turned. I wisht I could put dock burs in yo' pants!"

§ III

One morning in April Mrs. Blake arrived at the Mill House very early; she had been sent for soon after daybreak. She found her mother in the dining-room, awaiting her.

"Well, Rachel, it's come at last. They tell me she went very quietly. I want you to go through the linen-press and take what is needed. Open the green chest in the garret and find one of the embroidered nightgowns I used to wear when I was a girl. They'll be big enough for poor Jezebel now. If they're yellow with lying so long, Nancy can bleach one with alum and hang it in the sun. Will Saturday be soon enough for the funeral? The weather's not too warm?"

Her daughter agreed it was not. Mrs. Colbert motioned to the old man standing behind her chair. "Washington, tell Lizzie to come here."

In a few moments Lizzie appeared, having slipped on a clean apron and rubbed her face vigorously with the Master's rumpled breakfast napkin. She was barefoot, as usual, and was strug-

gling to swallow a last mouthful of batter-cake.
No matter at what hour she was sent for, she was
sure to be swallowing a last mouthful of something.

"Yes, Miss Sapphy?" Her hands were meekly
crossed over her clean apron.

"Lizzie, I expect you to do me credit this time.
I won't have any skimping for the watchers, as
there was when Manuel died."

Lizzie stared with astonishment and broke out
fervently.

"Lawd-a'mighty, Miss Sapphy! Jest as if I'd
think of bein' savin' fo' ole Aunt Jezebel! It never
would cross my thought! Why, dat Manuel was
jist a no-'count young boy, Missy."

"Boy or no boy, you put disgrace on me, and
it was talked about all up and down the Creek.
Cold batter-cakes and ponhos[1] for the watchers;
who ever heard of such stinginess! Now remember, there will be two nights to cook for. You are
to boil a ham and fry up plenty of middling meat.
Mrs. Blake will tell you how many loaves of light
bread[2] to bake, and there must be plenty of corn
bread, and sugar-cakes and ginger-cakes. Master
is going to invite all Mr. Lockheart's niggers to

[1] Scrapple.
[2] "Light" bread meant bread of wheat flour, in distinction
from corn bread.

come over and sit up, and likely some of Jezebel's grandchildren will come out from Winchester."

"Yes *mam!*" Lizzie rolled her eyes that shone like black-and-white china marbles. "Yes mam! I sho'ly will put my bes' foot for'ard fo' ole Aunt Jezebel an' all de yeahs she carry. But dat triflin' li'l Manuel wa'nt no 'count nohow, an' his pappy not much bettah — "

Mrs. Colbert held up her plump hand. "That will do, Lizzie. Remember this; if you don't do me credit at Jezebel's wake, I will send Bluebell back to Loudoun County for good, as sure as I sit here."

Lizzie put her two hands over her great bosom as if she were taking an oath. Sending Bluebell over to Loudoun County meant selling her there, and Lizzie knew it.

A few moments later Mrs. Blake, passing the kitchen on her way to Jezebel's cabin, heard Lizzie's malicious giggle. She stopped and looked in at the door. Lizzie was whispering to Bluebell, who sat drooping over the kitchen table, her elbows spread wide apart, as she sat day in and day out, supposedly helping her mother.

The Colberts, like all well-to-do families, had their own private burying-ground. It lay in a green field, and was enclosed by a wall, — flat slabs of brown stone laid one upon another, with a gate of wrought iron. A wide gravelled path divided the square plot in two halves. On one side were the family graves, with marble headstones. On the other side was the slaves' graveyard, with slate headstones bearing single names: "Dolly," "Thomas," "Manuel," and so on.

The mounds of masters and servants alike were covered with thick mats of myrtle. At this season innumerable sprays of new green shoots and starlike pale-blue blossoms shot out from the dark creeping vines which clung so close to the earth.

On Saturday afternoon the procession formed to carry Jezebel to the end of all her journeyings. Everyone was in black; the family, the neighbours from up and down the Creek, the Colbert negroes, and the slaves from down in the Hayfield country. Mrs. Blake's little girls had few dresses of any kind, so they were draped in black shawls lent by their grandmother. Mrs. Colbert herself wore the black crêpe she reserved for funerals. She was carried in her chair, and the miller, in his Sunday coat, walked beside her. They followed immediately behind the coffin, which was borne by four of Jezebel's great-grandsons, come out from Winchester.

While they stood about the grave, Mr. Fairhead
made a short address. He recalled Jezebel's long
wanderings; how she had come from a heathen
land where people worshipped idols and lived in
bloody warfare, to become a devout Christian and
an heir to all the Promises. Perhaps her long old
age had been granted her that she might fill out in
years the full measure of a Christian life. After
his last prayer, Lizzie and Bluebell sang " In the
Sweet By and By," and the company dispersed.
Jefferson and Washington, as the oldest servants,
stayed behind with the great-grandsons to fill up
the grave.

That night there was a big supper in the kitchen
for the Colbert negroes and all the visitors; a first
and second sitting at table. The darkies were always gay after a funeral, and this funeral had
pleased everyone. " Miss Sapphy sho'ly give Jezebel a beautiful laying away," they all agreed.

Washington, serving his master and mistress in
the big house, noticed that they, too, were more
animated than usual, expressing their satisfaction
that things had gone so well and that Jezebel's
young kinsmen had been able to come and carry
her. The Master sat long at table; had two help-
ings of pudding and drank four cups of tea. When
at last he rose, his wife said persuasively:

"Surely you don't mean to go back to the mill tonight, Henry, with your good clothes on."

"Yes, I think I must. I have been away all day. I want to speak to those boys from town and give them a little money. They will be starting back late tonight. Good night, Sapphira. I expect you are tired, and I hope you sleep well."

"The same to you," she said with a placid smile, which changed to an expression of annoyance while her eyes followed him to the door. As she sat there alone, her face grew hard and bitter. A few hours ago, when she was being carried out of the graveyard after the burial, she had seen something which greatly disturbed her. Behind the dark cedars just outside the stone wall, her husband and Nancy stood in deep conversation. The girl was in an attitude of dejection, her head hanging down, her hands clasped together, and the Master, whatever he was saying, was speaking very earnestly, with affectionate solicitude. Sapphira had put her handkerchief to her eyes, afraid that her face might show her indignation. Never before had she seen him expose himself like that. Whatever he was pressing upon that girl, he was not speaking as master to servant; there was nothing to suggest that special sort of kindliness permissible under such circumstances. He was not uttering condolences. It was personal. He had forgotten himself. Now, as she sat at the table, opposite his empty chair, she felt her anger rising. She rang her bell for the old butler.

"Washington, you may take me to my room. Send Till to me."

Till got Mrs. Colbert into her ruffled nightgown, and stood brushing out her heavy hair. She felt there was something wrong. She began to talk soothingly about the old days at Chestnut Hill. The Mistress scarcely heard her. As she walked toward her bed on Till's arm, she paused at the window, drew aside the long chintz curtains, and looked out toward the mill. There was a red patch in the darkness down there; the lights in the miller's room were burning. She let the curtain fall and continued her way to the wide four-post bed. Till said good-night, blew out the candles, and went away.

Left alone, the Mistress could not go to sleep. Her training and her own good sense had schooled her to know that there are very few situations in life worth getting wrought up about. But tonight she was angry. She was hurt — and remorseful. Because she was hurt, her mind kept going back to Chestnut Hill and her father. She wished she had been kinder to him in the years when he was crippled and often in pain. She wished she had shown him a little tenderness. His eyes used to ask for it sometimes, she remembered. She had been solicitous and resolutely cheerful; kept him up to the mark, saw that his body servant neglected nothing. But she knew there was something he wanted more than he wanted clean linen every morning, or to have his tea just as he liked it. She had never given in to him, never humoured his weakness. In those days she had not known the meaning of illness. To be crippled and incapacitated, not to come and go at will, to be left out of things as if one were in one's dotage — she had no realization of what that felt like, none at all. Invalids were to be kept clean and comfortable, greeted cheerily; that was their life.

The longer she lay awake thinking of those things in the far past, the more lonely and wretched and injured she felt herself to be tonight. Her usual fortitude seemed to break up altogether. She reached for it, but it was not there. Strange alarms and suspicions began to race through her mind. How far could she be deceived and mocked by her own servants in her own house? What was the meaning of that intimate conversation which had gone on under her very eyes this afternoon?

Unable to lie still any longer, she got cautiously out of bed, reaching for her cane and her armchair. Pushing the chair along beside her, she got to the window and again held back the curtain. The ruddy square of light still burned in the dark mill. She sat down in the chair and reflected. Hours ago she had heard Nancy put her straw tick outside the door. But was she there now? Perhaps she did not always sleep there. A substitute? — There were four young coloured girls, not counting Bluebell, who might easily take Nancy's place on that pallet. Very likely they did take her place, and everyone knew it. Could Till, even, be trusted? Besides, Till went early to her cabin — she would be the last to know.

The Mistress sat still, scarcely breathing, overcome by dread. The thought of being befooled, hoodwinked in any way, was unendurable to her. There were candles on her dressing-table, but she had no way to light them. Her throat was dry and seemed closed up. She felt afraid to call aloud, afraid to take a full breath. A faintness was coming over her. She put out her hand and resolutely rang her clapper bell.

The chamber door opened, and someone staggered in.

"Yes mam, yes mam! Whassa matter, Missy?"

Nancy's sleepy, startled voice. Mrs. Colbert dropped back in her chair and drew a long, slow breath. It was over. Her shattered, treacherous house stood safe about her again. She was in her own room, wakened out of a dream of disaster. — But she must see it through, what she had begun.

"Nancy, I'm taken bad. Run out to the kitchen and blow up the coals and put the kettle on. Then go for your mother. I must get my feet into hot water."

Nancy scurried down the long hall and out to the kitchen. She was wide awake now, and alarmed. She wasn't a girl to hold a grudge.

Till came, sooner than her mistress would have thought possible. Nancy brought the foot-tub and the big iron teakettle. Till sat on the floor rhythmically stroking her mistress's swollen ankles and knees, murmuring: "It's all right, Missy. They is no worse than common. It's just a chill you caught, waitin' out there by the graveside."

When the Mistress was again put to bed, Till begged to stay with her. But Mrs. Colbert, comforted by the promptness and sympathy of her servants, thanked them both, said the pain was gone now, and she would sleep better alone. As they helped her from her chair she had looked once more from her window: the miller's lights were still burning in the west room of the mill. Was the man worrying over some lawsuit he had never told her about, she wondered? Or was he, perhaps, reading his religious books? She knew he pondered at times upon how we are saved or lost. That was the disadvantage of having been raised a Lutheran. In her Church all those things had been decided long ago by heads much wiser than Henry's. She had married the only Colbert who had a conscience, and she sometimes wished he hadn't quite so much.

Behind the square of candlelight down there, the miller, in his mill clothes, was sitting with his Bible open on the table before him, but he was no longer reading. Jezebel's life, as Mr. Fairhead had summed it up, seemed a strange instance of predestination. For her, certainly, her capture had been a deliverance. Yet he hated the whole system of slavery. His father had never owned a slave. The Quakers who came down from Pennsylvania believed that slavery would one day be abolished. In the North there were many people who called themselves abolishers.

Henry Colbert knew he had a legal right to manumit any of his wife's negroes; but that would be an outrage to her feelings, and an injustice to the slaves themselves. Where would they go? How would they live? They had never learned to take care of themselves or to provide for tomorrow. They were a part of the Dodderidge property and the Dodderidge household. Of all the negro men on the place, Sampson, his head mill-hand, was the only one who might be able to get work and make a living out in the world. He was a tall, straight mulatto with a good countenance, thoughtful, intelligent. His head was full behind the ears, shaped more like a melon lying down than a peanut standing on end. Colbert trusted Sampson's judgment, and believed he could get a place for him among the Quaker mills in Philadelphia. He had considered buying Sampson from Sapphira and sending him to Pennsylvania a free man.

Three years ago he had called Sampson into his room one night, and proposed this plan to him. Sampson did not interrupt; he stood in his manly, responsible way, listening intently to his master. But when it was his turn to speak, he broke down. This was his home. Here he knew everybody. He didn't want to go out among strangers. Besides, Belle, his wife, was a slack worker, and his children were little. He could never keep them in a city as well off as they were here. What ever had put such a notion in Mister Henry's head? Wasn't he real smart about his work? Belle, he knew, wasn't much account to help down at the house, but she was good to the chillun, an' she didn't do no harm. Anyhow, he'd a'most sooner leave the chillun than leave the mill, when they'd got everything fixed up so nice and could bolt finer white flour than you could buy in town.

" I guess I'd miss you more than you'd miss the mill, Sampson. We'll say no more about it, if that's how you feel," said the miller, rising and putting his hand on Sampson's shoulder. There it ended. Sampson never afterward referred to this proposal, nor did his master.

On this night after Jezebel's burial, Henry Colbert had been reading over certain marked passages in the Book he accepted as a complete guide to human life. He had turned to all the verses marked with a large S. Joseph, Daniel, and the prophets had been slaves in foreign lands, and had brought good out of their captivity. Nowhere in his Bible had he ever been able to find a clear condemnation of slavery. There were injunctions of kindness to slaves, mercy and tolerance. *Remember them in bonds as bound with them.* Yes, but nowhere did his Bible say that there should be no one in bonds, no one at all. — And Henry had often asked himself, were we not all in bonds? If Lizzie, the cook, was in bonds to Sapphira, was she not almost equally in bonds to Lizzie?

The miller knew the hour must be getting late. His big silver watch he had left up at the house, on his wife's dressing-table. But he and the negroes could tell time by the stars. At this season of the year, if the Big Dipper had set under the dark spruce-clad hills behind Rachel's house, it would be past midnight. He opened his north window and looked out. Yes, the Dipper had gone down. The air of the soft, still, spring night came in at the window. There was no sound but the creek, pouring steadily over its rocky bottom. As he stood there, he repeated to himself some verses of a favourite hymn:

> God moves in a mysterious way
> His wonders to perform.

* * * * * * * *

> Deep in unfathomable mines
> Of never failing skill,
> He treasures up His bright designs
> And works His sovereign will.

We must rest, he told himself, on our confidence in His design. Design was clear enough in the stars, the seasons, in the woods and fields. But in human affairs — ? Perhaps our bewilderment came from a fault in our perceptions; we could never see what was behind the next turn of the road. Whenever he went to Winchester, he called upon a wise old Quaker. This man, though now

seventy, firmly believed that in his own lifetime
he would see one of those great designs accomplished; that the Lord had already chosen His heralds and His captains, and a morning would break
when all the black slaves would be free.

Book IV

SAPPHIRA'S DAUGHTER

BOOK IV

§ I

One breezy afternoon Mrs. Blake was footing it round the last loop of the " Double S," on her way to Timber Ridge. At the end of the steep grade she sat down on a mossy stump, took off her sunbonnet, and gave herself up to enjoyment of the spring day.

In the deep ravine below the road a mountain stream rushed coffee brown, throwing up crystal rainbows where it gurgled over rock ledges. On the steep hillside across the creek the tall forest trees were still bare, — the oak leaves no bigger than a squirrel's ear. From out the naked grey wood the dogwood thrust its crooked forks starred with white blossoms — the flowers set in their own wild way along the rampant zigzag branches. Their unexpectedness, their singular whiteness, never loses its wonder, even to the dullest dweller in those hills. In all the rich flowering and blushing and blooming of a Virginia spring, the scentless dogwood is the wildest thing and yet the most austere, the most unearthly.

Mrs. Blake was thinking this out to herself as she sat on the stump. She gave scarcely a glance at the wild honeysuckle all about her, growing low out of the gravelly soil, pink and rose colour, with long, trembling stamens which made each blossom look like a brilliant insect caught in flight. When at last she took her basket and travelled upward, she left the turnpike and followed a by-road along the crest of the Ridge. Up here the soil was better; planted fields and little green meadows lay along her path. May apples grew in the damp spots; their blossoms, like tiny pond lilies, gave out a heavy, almost sickening sweetness. Here and there stood a well-built farmhouse, with carefully tended yard and garden. Along the rail fences the locust trees were in bloom. The breeze caught their perfume and wafted it down the road. Every Virginian remembers those locusts which grow along the highways: their cloud-shaped masses of blue-green foliage and heavy drooping clusters of cream-white flowers like pea blossoms. Excepting the very old trees, the giants, the locusts look yielding and languid, like the mountain boy lounging against the counter when he goes to the country store. Yet, from the time they are big enough to cut, they make the toughest fence posts a farmer can find, and in the timber trade the yellow locust is valued for its resistance to moisture.

From the Ridge road Mrs. Blake could look down over hills and valleys, as if she were at the top of the world. She liked to go up there at any time of the year, and she liked to go on foot and alone. Even in her best days, before her husband died, when she lived in Washington and never came home to Back Creek for a visit, she used sometimes to be homesick for these mountains and the high places. This afternoon she was on the Ridge in answer to a sick call, but it was not a serious one, and she meant to enjoy herself.

Last evening a pale little girl, barefoot, in a carefully mended dress, had slipped silently into Mrs. Blake's kitchen without knocking. For all that her hair was braided and her face was washed, she was a distressful little creature, with dark circles about her eyes. There was something at once furtive and innocent in her face. She told Mrs. Blake how Granny let the flatiron fall on her foot t'other day, an' now her toe was festerin'. Would Miz Blake maybe come up an' see if they

ought to send for Doctor Brush? And now Mrs.
Blake was on her way to see. She had bandages
and turpentine ointment and arnica in her basket;
but she had also a fruit jar full of fresh-ground
coffee, half a baking of sugar cakes, and a loaf of
"light" bread. The poor folks on the Ridge es-
teemed coffee and wheat bread great delicacies.
This visit was not to be entirely wasted on a sore
foot. Indeed, Mrs. Blake suspected that the foot
was maybe not very bad, and that old Mrs. Ringer
had sent for her because she had not seen her for
a long time and wanted a visit with her.

Mrs. Blake herself looked forward to this visit.
Mrs. Ringer was better company than many people who were more fortunate; who came of better
blood, and had farms and raised sheep and pigs
for market. There were some families on the
Ridge who were comfortably off, owned a few
negroes to do the work, and held themselves very
high. If you called at the Pembertons', for instance, you were kept waiting half an hour in the
parlour while the ladies dressed and powdered
their faces. When at last they appeared, with
their mourning-bordered handkerchiefs and jet
earrings, they minded their manners so carefully
that the talk was very dull.

Now, Mandy Ringer had lived a hard life,
goodness knew, but misfortune and drudgery had

never broken her spirit. She was as thin as a grasshopper, and as lively as one. She had probably never spent a dull day. When she woke in the morning, she got into her calico dress in a flash and ran out to see what her garden had done overnight. Then she took a bucket and went to milk Sukey in the shed. Her son, though he was a cripple, would have done it for her, but in that country it was the custom for the women to do the milking. Mrs. Ringer wouldn't have trusted either of her two daughters to take care of Sukey. That little white-faced cow kept the log house going when everything else failed, and her calves brought in the only actual money the old woman ever saw.

Mrs. Ringer was born interested. She got a great deal of entertainment out of the weather and the behaviour of the moon. Any chance bit of gossip that came her way was a godsend. The rare sight of a strange face was a treat: a pedlar with a pack on his back, or a medicine-vendor come from across the Alleghenies with his little cart. Mrs. Ringer couldn't read or write, as she was frank to tell you, but the truth was she could read everything most important: the signs of the seasons, the meaning of the way the wood creatures behaved, and human faces. She once said to Mrs. Blake when they were talking things over:

" If the Lord'll jist let me stay alive, mam, an' not put me down into a dirty hole, I kin bear anything."

She had borne a good deal, certainly. Her son was a poor cripple, and both her daughters had been " fooled." That seldom occurred twice, even in the most shiftless households. Disgrace to the womenfolk brought any family very low in that country. But Mandy Ringer couldn't stay crushed for long. She came up like a cork, — probably with no better excuse than that the sun came up. Her spirits bubbled into the light like a spring and spread among the cresses.

Rachel Blake had always been drawn toward expansive, warm-hearted people. And she had known many such folks in her time, when she lived in Washington City before her husband died.

As she turned in at a low log house with a big outside rock chimney, Mrs. Ringer, her foot done up in rags, hopped lightly to the door to greet her.

" Now ain't you most a angel to come all the way up the hills to see us ! I declare I had a'most give you up, but Lawndis he tole me not to despair. An' he would go so fur as to shave fur you."

At this a brown-skinned man with a crooked back and a clubfoot came forward. " Yes, Miz

Blake, when the wind turned an' blowed the clouds
away, I reckoned you'd be along to see Mother."
His voice was mellow and grave, and there was
true courtesy in the way he looked at the visitor,
placed a chair for her, and relieved her of her
basket.

Mrs. Blake examined the sore foot and declared there was nothing worse than a bad bruise.
She applied her ointment and a clean bandage, and
took from her basket a pair of old carpet slippers.
"You'll be easy in these, Mrs. Ringer. Put them
on and keep them on. Don't on any account go
about barefoot. Now I'm a little weary after my
walk, and if Lawndis will kindle a fire I'm going
to make some coffee for us."

After the son had a fire going, he took up his
hat. "If you'll excuse me, Miz Blake, I'll go out
in the garden an' do some weedin'. You and
Mother'll feel freer to talk by yourselves. She
ain't seen much comp'ny lately." He limped out
of the house, careful not to put on his hat until
he was well outside the door.

Mrs. Ringer spread a white cloth on the
kitchen table and got out her blue chiney cups
and plates. Before the water was boiling Lawndis came back with a stone crock in his hands.
"Here, Mother. I seem to remember Miz Blake
don't like her coffee without cream. If you'll skim

some off, I'll take the crock back to the spring-house. We got a real cold springhouse, mam, bet-ter'n most folks up here. It's quite a piece away, but that's where the spring is."

"Your son surely has nice manners, Mrs. Ringer," remarked Mrs. Blake, as she watched him limping across the garden with the milk.

"Yes'm, Lawndis is a good boy, if I do say it. An' he gits a power a' work done, fur a lame man. Ain't it a pity I didn't have no luck with my gals?"

This was a delicate subject. Mrs. Blake did not wish to discuss it. "Where are the girls today?" she asked politely, as if there were nothing queer about them.

"Ginnie, she's got work up at Capon Springs, helpin' clean the hotel fur summer visitors. Up there they ain't heered about her trouble, maybe. I don't know where Marge is this minute, but she's likely off in the woods some'ers, 'shamed to have you see her. It would all a-been different, Miz Blake, if my Lawndis was a strong man. Then he could a-tracked down the fellers an' fit with 'em, an' made 'em marry his sisters. But them raskels knowed my pore gals hadn't nobody to stand up fur 'em. Fellers is skeered to make free with a gal that's got able men folks to see she gits her rights."

Mrs. Blake still sought to avoid discussing these

misfortunes, since there was nothing she could do to remedy them. She said blandly: " Well, whatever happened, I know Lawndis would never be hard on his sisters. Now do tell me, Mrs. Ringer, who did you name your boy after? I've often wondered, and never thought to ask you."

"Lawndis? Why, after the preacher. Can't you remember, when you was a little girl there come a preacher a-holdin' revivals through these parts? He held meetin's every night fur a week an' more at Bethel Church, an' I never missed a sermon. I ain't never heered sich sermons before nor since. When the next baby come, I called him after that preacher."

Yes, Mrs. Blake remembered the preacher; he wore a long-tailed coat, even on horseback, and his name was Leonidas Bright. The hill people could do queer things with unfamiliar names.

At this moment the pale little girl who had come to Mrs. Blake's yesterday stole down the ladder from the loft over the kitchen and shyly approached the table. In her hand was a little wooden box full of quartz crystals she had picked up on the stony hillsides.

" Is these di'monds, Miz Blake, mam? Kin I sell 'em fur money?"

" No, child, I'm afraid they're not diamonds. They're just as pretty, though."

"Now, Becky, what need you come troublin'
Miz Blake fur? I tole you they ain't di'monds.
You run back upstairs an' mind the baby, an'
here's a cake fur you Miz Blake fetched me. Is
he asleep?"

"Yes'm."

Mrs. Blake slipped the child a second cake, and
she went noiselessly up the ladder.

The grandmother gave a cackling little laugh.
"That's the fashion up here now. Since the
Bethel robbery everybody thinks they kin make
a fortin sellin' somethin'. It's come down even to
pore Becky."

"What robbery are you talkin' about, Mrs.
Ringer?"

Mrs. Ringer put down the cup halfway to her
lips. "You ain't meanin' you never heered of the
Bethel communion service bein' stole?"

"I surely never heard a word about it."

Mrs. Ringer's face glowed. "Well, I'm su'-
prised, mam! It's a disgrace to us all up here, an'
we can't hardly talk of nothin' else. Last Sunday
night, after preachin', the whole communion service, the silver plate an' the silver goblet an' the
little pitchers, was taken. An' now his triflin' relations is tryin' to put it off on Casper Flight, as good
a boy as ever lived, because he has the door key
so he kin sweep out the church an' keep it clean.

Now we all know a winder was broke out the night the deed was done, so what has Casper's key got to do with it, I'd like to know? Would he break a winder, when he had a key? "

Mrs. Blake was thoroughly interested. " You mean the Flight boy that comes to Mr. Fairhead's school? Why, his teacher can't say enough good of him."

" That's him I mean. He's bein' persecuted by them louts of cousins of his'n, them ugly Keyser boys that runs a still. Who's they to act up for the church, when they was never inside one? Unless "—here Mrs. Ringer paused and shook her finger at Mrs. Blake as she added impressively —"unless they was inside Bethel Church last Sunday night, after meetin'."

" But why are the Keysers trying to put it on Casper? You say they're cousins."

" Now, Miz Blake, who kin hate worse'n cousins? We all know that. They hates him jist on account of his bein' a good boy, and tryin' to make somethin' of hisself, walkin' all the way down to Back Creek to learn to read an' write. Nobody in their fam'ly could ever read 'n' write, an' damned if anybody ever will. It's pure spite, an' I tell Lawndis I know Buck Keyser broke that winder an' clomb in an' robbed the Lord, as well as if I'd seen him do it. He's got them things hid away some'ers, an' one day he'll tromp over the Alleghenies where he ain't knowed, an' sell 'em."

Mrs. Blake sniffed audibly. "Well, he won't get much for 'em. That Bethel communion set ain't silver at all. It's plated stuff, and poor plate at that, I can tell you."

Mrs. Ringer started in her chair. "Is that so, Miz Blake! Now, nobody but you would a-knowed. Lordy me, I wisht I could a-had your chance, mam. It's city life that learns you, an' I'd a-loved it! So with all their deviltry they ain't got no fortin hid away, an' fur all the talk they've raised, it don't amount to much more'n pore Becky's di'monds! There is a kind-a justice in this world after all, now ain't there?"

Their talk turned naturally to the classic example of belated justice: the murder of the pedlar at the red brick house on the Ridge Road, and its exposure after twenty years. While Mrs. Ringer was telling all she remembered of the two wretched women who had killed the pedlar for his pack, Lawndis appeared at the door, sweaty and panting.

"Maw, I'm afeered them Keysers is got Casper. I heered trouble over in the woods, an' Buck's big haw-haw. He's got the meanest laff ever was, when he's out fur devilment. I'm a-goin' over."

Mrs. Ringer sprang up. "Then I'm a-goin' with ye."

"No you ain't, Maw. You're lamed with your foot."

"I reckon I'm no lamer'n you air. Come along, Miz Blake, we'll all go. They ain't no business in our woods."

Mrs. Blake picked up her basket. "Take one of Lawndis' canes, Mandy, and spare your foot all you can." She set out with the two cripples, down the garden, past the springhouse, and over toward the wood where they heard ugly, taunting voices.

They had not gone far when they came upon the three Keysers and their captive. A young boy, perhaps fifteen or sixteen, was stripped naked to the waist and bound tight to a chestnut sapling. Three men were lounging about the tree making fun of him. The brother called Buck had his sleeves rolled up and his shirt open, showing a thick fleece of red hair on his chest and forearms. He was laughing and cracking a lash of plaited cowhide thongs. The boy tied to the tree said not a word in answer to Buck's taunting questions. He made no sound at all, did not even look up when Mrs. Blake came swishing through the bushes. For all he had set his teeth tight together, she could see his lower jaw trembling.

Mrs. Ringer spoke first. "Now what air you Keysers up to?"

Big Buck had a very smooth way with him when he took the trouble. He had certainly not expected to see Mrs. Blake from Back Creek, and her appearance put a different light on things. He pulled off his hat and spoke easy.

"Nothin' but a fam'ly matter, folks. This young feller's been charged with takin' the communion set. His maw's a Keyser, an' it's fur us to settle with him. You know yourselves his paw's no account, an' that Baptist preacher he goes to school to don't seem to a-learned him to keep his hands off things. Time fur the fam'ly to learn him a little. He's got to tell where them things is hid."

Mrs. Blake had kept a steady eye on Buck, and now she spoke.

"Then you'd better go and get 'em, Buck Keyser, and put 'em back where they belong, for they're poor plated stuff, and you'll get nothing for them but trouble."

Buck's face didn't change, but his two brothers looked at each other.

"That's what I'm after doin', Miz Blake, onct I git 'em out-a him." With that he swung his lash and gave Casper a cut on the bare shoulder. The boy made no sound, but poor Lawndis was so worked upon that he burst out crying and threw his arms round the prisoner to shield him with his own back. "Don't you dast hit him agin! I can't fight ye, I'm jist a pore mock of a man, but you'll have to finish me afore you tech him."

Mrs. Blake knew Lawndis would be sick for a week after such an outbreak. "Shame on you, Buck Keyser!" she said, going up to him and putting her hand on his hairy arm. "It's Lawndis will get the most punishment out of this, and you know it. What did you come on their place for, to act your foolishness? What have you got against Lawndis?"

"We ain't got nothing agin Lawndis. This whimperin' boy come hidin' in the Ringer woods, 'cause he's a coward an' can't take a lickin'. We was after him, an' come on him here, that's how. Don't act the fool, Lawndis. I'll take care of my kin some'ers out-a your woods. He'll git his ticklin' when there's no ladies around. Come on, boys. Good day to you, Miz Blake."

Mrs. Blake told Lawndis to go back to the house and drink the coffee that was left. While the two women untied the Flight boy and hunted for his shirt, Mrs. Ringer whispered: "Like as not they brought him into our woods a purpose. They was feelin' devilish, an' what's the good a-actin' devilish if nobody sees you? They knows Lawndis is soft that-a-way, an' can't see a sparrer fall. It's a mercy you was here, Miz Blake. I reckon they don't want to git in too bad with your Paw."

On her way down the "Double S" and the "holler" road, Mrs. Blake told herself she must have a talk with David Fairhead about Casper. Perhaps it wasn't wise to encourage him. "I don't know whether that boy's strong enough to master what's around him," she said to herself. "A man's got to be stronger'n a bull to get out of the place he was born in. I just hope I won't dream tonight the way Casper stood against that tree, with his lower jaw tremblin'."

§ II

To see Mrs. Blake working about her house and garden, a stranger would scarcely guess that she had lived the happiest years of her life in Washington, and had known a wider experience of the world than her more worldly mother.

Rachel was sixteen years old when Michael Blake rode through Frederick County soliciting votes. He was already a member of the Virginia State Legislature, and was a nominee for the United States Congress. He spent some days at the Mill Farm, where he was warmly welcomed. Henry Colbert approved of Blake's record and his principles, and the Mistress was charmed by his good manners, his handsome face and blue eyes. When he said good-bye and rode up into the Capon River country, she missed him.

In two weeks he came back to the Mill Farm. He had made up his mind. He had made it up, indeed, on his first visit, but he had disclosed his intentions to no one, not even to Rachel. When, on this second visit, he asked the miller and Sapphira for their daughter's hand, they were speechless from astonishment. After the interview in which they gave their consent, Mrs. Colbert retired to her room and bolted the door for an hour to regain her composure.

She had never hoped for anything so good for Rachel. She had often doubted whether she would succeed in getting her married at all. Two older daughters she had married very well. But she could see nothing in this girl likely to be attractive to young men. Rachel was well-enough looking, in her father's masterful way, but no one could call her pretty. She was reserved to a degree which her mother called sullenness, and she had decided opinions on matters which did not concern women at all. She was her father's favourite; that was natural, since she was just like him. But this happy, fair-complexioned young Blake, with his warm laugh and mellow voice — Well, Mrs. Colbert reflected, there is no accounting for tastes. Blake was Irish, and the Irish often leap before they look.

When she had recovered herself, Mrs. Colbert sat down to write the amazing news to her sisters.

While she was at her desk, the young man was with Rachel. He had found her in the flower garden, separating tufts of clove pinks. He wiped her hands on his handkerchief and led her into the lilac arbour. Seated beside her on the rustic bench, he told her his story in the manner of the period.

On the first night of his first visit, he said, when he sat opposite her at the supper table, it all happened. He had watched her face in the candle-light and found it hard to reply to her mother's friendly questions, or to keep his mind on the conversation. He had stayed on at the house until he was afraid he might wear out his welcome. After he rode away, he could think of nothing but Rachel whenever he was alone. He was thirty years old, and had never before met a girl whom he wished to marry. Indeed, he admitted, he " liked his liberty." Now everything was different. Her father and mother had given their consent. But he must have her own, spoken from the heart.

" Do you think you could come to love me, really love me, Rachel? " His voice was wistful, almost sad.

She looked up and met his blue eyes fearlessly, something intense flashed into her own. " I do already, Michael."

" My sweetheart! May I have one kiss? "

She put her hands on his shoulders, holding him back, and with that almost fierce devotion still shining in her eyes said pleadingly: " Please, Michael, please! Not until the words have been said."

No reply could have made him happier. He caught her two hands and buried his face in them.

This was in the eighteen-thirties, when loose manners were very loose, and the proprieties correspondingly strict. Young bachelors who were free in their morals were very exacting that the girl they chose for a wife should be virginal in mind as well as in body. The worst that could be said of an unmarried girl was that " she knew too much."

Immediately after Michael's election as Representative for the —th District, the young couple were married and went to Washington to live in a small rented house. The devotion Michael read in Rachel's eyes when she refused him the betrothal kiss soon became her whole life: there was nothing of her left outside it. In every sense he was her first love. More than that, he had taken her from a home where she had never been happy. She felt for him all that was due to a rescuer and a saviour. Until he came, her heart was cold and frozen.

When Rachel was twelve years old, she had chanced to overhear a conversation which coloured her thoughts and feelings ever afterward. In those days she used often to walk to the post office to get the mail, although she knew this annoyed her mother. Rachel was deeply attached to the post-mistress, then a young woman who had lately been left a widow with three little boys. One morning she was sitting on Mrs. Bywaters's shady front porch, behind the blooming honeysuckle vines, when she saw a handsome old gentleman ride up to the hitch-post, dismount, and tie his horse. That was Mr. Cartmell, Mrs. Bywaters's father. As he walked up the gravel path to the porch steps, his daughter saw him and came out to greet him. They went into the house together, leaving the door open behind them. Rachel liked to listen to Mr. Cartmell; his talk had a flavour of old-fashioned courtesy.

"I came with something on my mind today, daughter," he began. "Your mother and I think you have it too hard up here, since Jonah went. What with looking after the mail, and attending to your children and the housework, there is too much for one woman to do. Our old neighbour, Mr. Longfield, tells me he is willing to part with one of Abigail's daughters. But he would never sell her off to strangers. In busy seasons your mother often hires her from the Longfields, and finds her capable and willing. I would like to buy Mandy for you, and bring her up here myself. You would have a smart girl to help you, and she would have a good home."

There was a pause. Then Mrs. Bywaters said:
"Could we hire Mandy from the Longfields
for a couple years, maybe?"

"I made such a proposal to Mr. Longfield, but
he needs a considerable sum of money at once. He
is forced to sell Mose, his body servant, into Winchester. You will remember our neighbour was
somewhat inclined to extravagance. He has got
behind."

Another pause. "You have never owned any
slaves yourself, Father," she said thoughtfully, as
if considering.

"You know my feeling on that matter, Caroline.
But down with us, in the Round Hill neighbourhood, it is always easy to hire help from farmers
who have too many negroes. Up here there are
few slave-owners, and a raw white girl from the
mountains would be of little help to you."

This time there was no pause. Mrs. Bywaters
spoke quietly but firmly. "It's kindly thought of
you, Father, and kindly spoken. But neither you
nor I have ever owned flesh and blood, and I will
not begin it. I am young and strong, and I'll make
shift to manage. Peace of mind is what I value
most."

Little Rachel Colbert, sitting breathless on the
porch, heard Mr. Cartmell rise from his squeaky
splint-bottom chair and say: "You are my own

daughter, Caroline. We will manage." The deep
emotion in his voice, and the hush which followed,
made Rachel realize that she had been eavesdrop-
ping, listening to talk that was private and personal. She fled swiftly through the yard and out
to the road. Her feet must have found the way
home, for she gave no heed to where she was going. A feeling long smothered had blazed up in
her — had become a conviction. She had never
heard the thing said before, never put into words.
It was the *owning* that was wrong, the relation itself, no matter how convenient or agreeable it
might be for master or servant. She had always
known it was wrong. It was the thing that made
her unhappy at home, and came between her and
her mother. How she hated her mother's voice in
sarcastic reprimand to the servants! And she
hated it in contemptuous indulgence. Till and
Aunt Jezebel were the only blacks to whom her
mother never spoke with that scornful leniency.

After that morning on Mrs. Bywaters's porch,
Rachel was more than ever reserved and shut
within herself. Her two aunts disapproved of her;
she dreaded the yearly visit to them. At home,
she knew that all the servants were fond of her
mother, in good or ill humour, and that they were
not fond of her. She was not at all what the darkies thought a young lady should be. Till's good

manners were barely sufficient to conceal her dis-
appointment in Miss Sapphy's youngest daughter.

Michael Blake had dropped from the clouds,
as it were, to deliver Rachel from her loneliness,
from life in a home where she had not a single con-
fidant. She often wondered how she had borne
that life at all. Once settled in the narrow rented
house on R Street, she no longer brooded upon
real or imagined injustices. Her mind and energy,
and she was endowed with both, were wholly given
to making for Michael the kind of home he
wanted, and doing it on very little money.

Representative Blake was, he admitted, " fond
of the pleasures of the table." Rachel became ex-
pert in cookery. Everything he liked, done as he
liked, appeared in season on his dinner table. He
lunched at an oyster bar near the Capitol, and
dined at eight in the evening. His wife had the
whole day to prepare his favourite dishes. She put
herself under the instruction of a free mulatto
woman from New Orleans, whose master had
manumitted her when he was dying in Washington. Sarah now made her living by cooking for
dinner parties.

Every morning, on his way to the Capitol, Michael stopped at the big market and sent home
the choicest food of the season. In those days the

Washington markets were second to none in the world for fish and game: wild ducks, partridges, pheasants, wild turkeys . . . the woods were full of wildfowl. The uncontaminated bays and rivers swarmed with fish: Potomac shad, Baltimore oysters, shrimps, scallops, lobsters, and terrapin. In the spring the Dutch truck gardeners brought in the first salads and asparagus and strawberries.

A group of Louisiana planters who came to Washington every winter kept Michael's cellar supplied with good wines. These Southerners often dined at the Blakes', grateful for an escape from the bleakness of Washington hotels. They usually brought with them a young French officer who had some humble post at the French Legation. Too poor to marry, Chénier lived wretchedly in a boarding-house. His devotion to Mrs. Blake and her good dinners became a positive embarrassment, the subject of many a jest at Michael's breakfast table.

The planters came up to Washington unaccompanied by their families. At the round dinner table in the Blakes' narrow dining-room would be seated five or six men, never more than seven, in broadcloth and shining linen. The Louisianians wore frilled shirts with diamond studs, the officer his shabby dress uniform. There was no place set for a woman, not even for the hostess. The hostess was below stairs in the brick-floored basement kitchen. Her companions were the glowing coal range, a sink with a hydrant pump, shelves of copper cooking vessels, and an adjacent "cold pantry" full of food and drink. There she achieved a dinner for epicures, with no help but Sarah, the mulatto, who also served in the dining-room.

At the end of the dinner, when the dessert had been carried up by the stately mulatto, then there was a call for the hostess. Slipping off her long white apron and dashing a little powder over her face, Rachel went upstairs to drink a glass of champagne with the guests. If she did not appear soon after the dessert, the young Frenchman ran down to the kitchen and brought her up on his arm. Her husband and his friends rose to toast her. Hot and flushed as she was, their faces by this time were quite as rosy, and, to their slightly contracted pupils, the young woman who had given them such a dinner was beautiful.

Rachel enjoyed the iced wine and the warm praise, — and she enjoyed the gaiety. For after she joined the party, it became distinctly gayer, however lively it had been before. She sat in Michael's chair, and he stood behind her, filled her glass, and coaxed her to eat his dessert, beaming with his pride in her.

After the first glass she did not feel tired. Her

responsibilities over, she relaxed and leaned back in Michael's big chair, laughing at the funny stories, — her father's deep laugh. She begged them to sing for her, "Little Brown Jug" and "Auld Lang Syne." Like many persons of a serious temper, she loved being with people who were easily and carelessly merry.

In due time the children came along; first a son, Robert, the well-beloved. A second boy died in infancy. Then came the two girls, Mary and Betty. During those happy years Rachel had but one anxiety: her husband's extravagant tastes and his carelessness about keeping the tradesmen paid up. Michael reassured her as to the future. He carried what he termed "a heavy life insurance," used to show her the premium cheques before he sent them off. In the months before a new baby came, there was no entertaining, and Rachel was able to cut the household expenses, — though Michael largely defeated her thrift by bringing her presents.

Even in those years there was something of the devotee in Rachel. The will to self-abnegation which showed itself later was in her then, though it took the form of untiring service to a man's pleasure and of almost idolatrous love for her first-born. Perhaps she was conscious of a certain chill in her own nature and was afraid of being insufficient to her pleasure-loving husband. His rich enjoyment of life had an irresistible charm for her.

Rachel had been married thirteen years when Michael thought he could afford to accept the long-pressed invitation of his Southern friends to visit them in New Orleans. He persuaded his wife to let him take the boy along with him. Robert was then eleven, handsome and gay like his father. Rachel knew the trip would be a fine experience for him; she ought not to hold him back. She went to Baltimore to see them sail. When the last whistle blew, and the steamboat began to move out into the bay, she could see Michael standing in the stern, and beside him the boy, waving his new Scotch cap with ribands.

Letters came often; those from Robbie were especially cherished. The date of their return was fixed, but they did not come by the boat on which Rachel expected them. There was something in the newspapers about an epidemic down there, but it was immediately denied. After Mrs. Blake had waited through an anxious fortnight, a visitor knocked at her door, — one of the old New Orleans friends who had come up to Washington to tell her what he could not write. Only the day before Michael was to start for home, the boy fell ill. His father, who never left him for a moment, would not believe it was yellow fever, until the child began to vomit black blood. Forty-eight hours afterward Michael Blake himself died of the contagion. They were both buried in the Protestant cemetery in New Orleans.

Henry Colbert first learned of his son-in-law's death from a paragraph in the Baltimore *Sun*, — the paper was already a week old. He went at once to Winchester and took the train for Washington. He found Rachel in her bed, the daylight shut out, her door locked. She had refused to admit her doctor and Michael's lawyer. Sarah, the mulatto woman, had come to stay in the house and was taking care of the two children.

The miller put his shoulder under the wheel. Michael's life-insurance policy had lapsed; the last two premiums had not been paid. There was little left for the widow but her furniture and a few debts. Blake's friends made up a generous purse for her. Henry Colbert paid off the creditors and brought Rachel and her children home to Back Creek. They stayed at the Mill Farm while Mr. Whitford built the house by the road in which Mrs. Blake had lived ever since.

During the months when the house was a-building the miller and his wife grew very fond of Mary and Betty. Mrs. Colbert's relations with her daughter were pleasanter than they had ever been before. To be sure, there were things in the past which she could not forget. Gravest of them was that Rachel had not once invited her mother, then not an invalid but a very active woman, to come to Washington to visit her. Among Virginians such a slight could never be forgiven. That Mrs. Blake's city house was small and cramped was no excuse. Your near kin were expected to entertain you, even though they had to sleep on cots in the hall and give you their sleeping-chamber. To be in Washington, visitors would cheerfully put up with any discomfort. That your own daughter lived there, and you did not visit her, required explanation to your relatives and friends.

When Rachel came back to the Mill Farm, widowed and poor, her mother found it easier to overlook past differences than she would have done a few years before. Mrs. Colbert's illness had not yet come upon her, but she had had warnings. Already she had given over horseback riding, though women of that time often kept to the saddle when they were well in their seventies.

During the six years that had gone by since Mrs. Blake's return, the Back Creek people had grown used to seeing her come and go along the roads and mountain paths, on her way to some house where misfortune had preceded her. If a neighbour, unable to restrain curiosity, asked any question about how people lived in Washington, she replied simply:

"I hardly remember. All that is gone. I'd take it kindly of you not to bring it back to me. This is my home now, and I want to live here like I had never gone away."

The postmistress, whom she had so loved as a child, was the only neighbour with whom she ever talked freely. They were drawn together by deep convictions they had in common.

Mrs. Bywaters, though she was poor, subscribed for the New York *Tribune*. Since she was in Government employ, this was an indiscreet thing to do. Even her father, Mr. Cartmell, thought it unwise. The papers came to her heavily wrapped and addressed in ink. She kept them locked in her upper bureau drawer and often gave Mrs. Blake interesting numbers to carry home in her basket. They were handy to start a fire with, she said.

Book V

MARTIN COLBERT

BOOK V

§ I

On the first day of June the Romney stage, more than an hour late, crossed Back Creek and stopped before the tollgate. A girl with a broad, flat, good-natured face came out to lift the rickety gate and collect the toll. The driver leaned down from his high seat to pass the time of day with her. This courtesy he never omitted, no matter how much he was behind in his schedule. While the driver was chatting, one of his five passengers jumped out at the rear end of the stage: a young man, well dressed and good-looking. He walked forward and interrupted.

"I say, driver, isn't that turn-off the road to the mill?"

"Shorely is, sir."

"Then I'll walk over from here. Take my trunk on to the post office, please, and leave it. My uncle will send for it."

"Your uncle?"

"Yes; Mr. Colbert, at the mill."

"So that's how it is; you're a Colbert." The driver shifted his tobacco to the other cheek. "Which on 'em is your paw?"

"Jacob. I'm Martin Colbert."

"Is that so!" He looked the young man over with interest. "Ever been out here before?"

"Yes, when I was a youngster. Good day, driver. Don't forget to put my trunk off." The young man saw no reason for tarrying; there was no one in sight but the toll-girl, noticeable only for her flat red face. Martin lifted his hat to her, however, and set off down the stony by-road before the stage started. The driver leaned over to say to the girl: "The miller won't be none too tickled to see him, I reckon! Feller must 'a' got into some scrape agin, or he wouldn't be comin' out here, with a trunk, too! He's a turrible wild one."

The stage rattled on toward the post office, where it was to change horses. The flat-faced girl turned and went slowly down the mill road after the stranger, peering to right and left; but he was already hidden from sight by the tall sassafras bushes which grew thick all along the rail fence.

Young Colbert walked along carelessly, finding exercise agreeable after the jolting of the stage. Sometimes he hummed a tune, sometimes he chuckled and ducked his shoulders. He was amused to find himself actually on his way to the Mill House, one of the dreariest spots in all Virginia, he reckoned. "The joke's on me," his giggle seemed to say.

Just now he was lucky to have any place to go where he would be comfortable and well fed, and rid of his creditors. He was a tall, well-enough built fellow, but there was something soft about the lines of his body. He carried himself loosely at the shoulders and thighs. His clothes were town clothes, but strolling along unobserved he behaved like a country boy. When he laughed at his present predicament, he hitched up his trousers by his gallowses where his waistcoat hung open. He was easily diverted; no fixed purpose lurked behind his chuckle, though there was sometimes a flash of slyness in his whisky-coloured eyes. He stopped to watch a mud-turtle waddle across the road, and rolled the old fellow over on his back to see him kick — then relented and turned him right side up. When he got near the mill, Martin buttoned his waistcoat, wiped the dust from his face, and straightened his shoulders. He did not stop at the mill, but went directly on to the house. Till met him at the front door with genuine cordiality, restrained by correctness.

"The Mistress is waiting for you in the parlour, Mr. Martin. We expected you before this."

"Sorry, Till. The stage was late starting; had to wait for passengers from Martinsburg. All the folks well here?"

"They're all as usual, sir." She opened the door into the parlour, where Mrs. Colbert was sitting near the fireplace, now closed by a painted fire-board. She smiled graciously and held out her hand. Martin hurried across the room, and gallantly kissed her on the cheek.

She shook her finger at him. "You've kept me waiting for you a long while, Martin. You were certainly in no hurry to make me a visit. I first wrote you before Easter, and here we are coming into June."

"It's been a right busy time on the place, Aunt Sapphy." He was still standing beside her chair. She reached out and felt his palm. "I don't find any calluses."

He laughed gaily. "Oh, we have plenty of field-hands — too many!"

Washington came in with the tea-tray and put it on the table beside the Mistress. The visitor drew up a chair and sat down opposite his aunt,

crossing his legs and falling into an attitude of
easy indolence which diverted her. She liked a
dash of impudence in young men whom she considered attractive; and Martin, she was thinking,
was the best favoured of the younger Colberts.
Just then she happened to notice that his boots
were very dusty.

" Why, Martin, didn't you ride your mare
out? "

" No, ma'am. I came on the stage and walked
over from the tollgate."

" The stage? You must have been very uncom-
fortable. Why didn't you ride Merrylegs, and
send your box by the stage? It's a pleasant ride.'*

" I sold Merrylegs this spring. Had a good of.
fer and needed the money."

While he helped himself to sandwiches she
studied his face.

" Are you sure you sold her, Mart? " she asked
shrewdly.

He had not expected this question. He gave
her a quick glance, and ducked his head with a grin
which seemed to say: " You've caught me now! "

" Well, anyhow, I parted with her, Aunt Sapphy."

" Cards, I'll be bound! "

" No, honour bright. It was a racing bet. I'm
not much of a card man. But I lose my head at the

races." He looked at her frankly, holding out his teacup with an "If you please." Easy, confidential, a trifle free in manner, as if she were not an old woman and an invalid. That was how she liked it. She told herself that Martin's visit would be very refreshing. She almost believed she had urged him to come solely because she liked to have young people about.

"No matter. We can let you have a mount. Henry keeps a good riding horse to go in to Winchester on business. He doesn't like to be bothered with the carriage. I always preferred to go on horseback when I went to town for Sunday service."

"You pretty nearly lived on horseback, didn't you? Oh, down with us they still tell about how you used to take the fences."

"Yes, I liked riding, but I never gave myself over body and soul to horses, as the Bushwells appear to do."

"That's right. They just live for the stables. The house and grounds would shock you now. People say they used to keep the place up as long as you went to visit there. But Chestnut Hill has never been the same since old Matchem died."

Till appeared at the door and said that Martin's box had come.

Mrs. Colbert beckoned her. "Call Nancy to

take Mr. Martin up to his room and unpack his things for him. She keeps your uncle's room at the mill, Martin, and she will do yours, and look after your laundry. Young men are none too orderly, I seem to remember. Now I will rest for an hour before supper."

Martin went up the wide staircase leading from the long hall. Upstairs he saw an open door, and a young mulatto girl standing at attention outside.

"And are you Nancy? Good evening, Nancy. I hear you are going to take care of me." He stood still and looked hard at her.

A wave of pink went over her gold-coloured cheeks, and her eyes fell. "If I can please you, sir," she said quietly, waiting for him to enter the chamber.

"Oh, you do please me!" he laughed.

Going into the room, Martin glanced about: large, airy, not too much furniture, canopy bed with fresh muslin curtains. He opened one of the front windows and looked out over the yard, the mill, the woods across the creek. Beyond the woods the blue, wavy slopes of the North Mountain lay against the sky. The upper porch ran along outside the room; he put one leg out through the open window. "Am I allowed to go on the veranda, girl? Very strict rules in this house, I've heard tell."

"Certainly, sir. There's a door in the hall goes out to the upper porch," she said quickly, correcting an implied reproach on the house.

Martin drew in his foot. "That will be more convenient. And now you can unpack my trunk."

"It's locked, sir."

"Lordy, I forgot!" His sole-leather trunk had been placed on a chair. He unlocked it and threw back the lid. "There. Now you put my clothes where you think they ought to go, and I'll watch you, so I'll know where to find them." He pulled off his coat and waistcoat, threw them on the bed, and sat down in the usual guest-chamber rocking-chair. Nancy took the discarded upper garments and hung them in the clothes-press. She opened the bureau drawers and stood timidly hesitating before the trunk.

"Would you like your collars an' neckcloths kept in the upper drawer, sir?"

He was just lighting a cigar. "Follow your own notion. We have a slut of a housekeeper at home. I never know where to find anything."

She went noiselessly to work, moving back and forth between the bureau and the press. Young Colbert sat with his feet on the low window sill, enjoying his cigar.

"Does my aunt object to smoking?" he asked presently.

"Oh, no, sir! She likes to have the gen'lemen smoke."

After putting away the shirts and nightshirts, Nancy lifted the top tray and stood perplexed by the confusion she found below.

"If you don't mind, sir, I'll take the coats an' pants downstairs direc'ly, an' press 'em."

"That's a good idea."

The shoes and boots she found stuffed full of dirty socks and soiled underwear. She made a bundle of the rumpled linen and put it outside the door. She was embarrassed because the guest watched her so closely.

"Anybody ever tell you you're a damned pretty girl, Nancy?" she heard as she stooped over the trunk.

"No, sir."

Martin would have done better to change his tone. But he did not see her face, and went on teasingly:

"You tryin' to make me believe none of these country jakes around here been makin' up to you? You can't fool me!"

"There's good, kind folks on Back Creek, Mr. Martin."

"You don't say, honey!" Martin laughed, stretching his loose shoulders.

Nancy didn't like his laugh, not at all! She took

up an armful of coats and trousers, snatched the pile of soiled linen outside the door, and vanished so quickly that when the young man turned from throwing his cigar end out of the window, he was amazed to find her gone.

§ II

Mrs. Colbert had Zack sent down to the mill to ask her husband to come up early before supper-time. When his wife told him that his nephew had come to visit them, he showed neither pleasure nor annoyance. Hospitality, in those days, was one of the decencies of life. Whoever came, friend or stranger, was made welcome and cared for according to his place in the world. Henry saw that his wife was wearing her velvet gown, so he unquestioningly changed his shirt and put on his black suit. When Martin came downstairs, his uncle met him in the spacious hall, gave him a hearty handshake, and told him he was glad to see him.

Washington announced supper and wheeled the Mistress to her place at table. The miller noticed that a bottle of his best Madeira was on the sideboard. As soon as the two men were seated, Washington filled the wineglasses. Martin lifted his, saying:

" To the lady of the house, Uncle Henry," bowing to his aunt, who smiled graciously. His uncle also smiled.

Supper was served at seven o'clock in summer, and throughout the hour Sampson's twelve-year-old Katie, barefoot, in a stiffly starched red calico dress, walked round and round the table waving a long flybrush made of a peacock's tail. Even in town houses the flybrush was part of the table service.

Katie had seldom heard such animated conversation at supper. Mrs. Colbert had reserved all her inquiries about Loudoun County families until her husband should be present. She wished Martin to make a good impression. He was full of gossip and told a story well. He complimented his uncle on his wine, and drank it liberally. The abstemious miller drank two glasses and left the third standing full. His wife, who always had a little wine with her supper, signalled Washington to bring on another bottle.

Martin's stories were never quite indecent, and always characteristic of old Loudoun County neighbours. When he was talking about Captain Bushwell's fine horses, he happened to say: " Fact is, his trainers say nowadays Bushwell sleeps in the stables." Suddenly remembering that the miller was said to sleep at the mill, he caught himself up with a giggle, blushed, and ducked his shoulders.

Sapphira promptly covered his blush by asking

him about Hal Gogarty, a dare-devil young Irishman whose stables rivalled Bushwell's.

"Gogarty? 'Course you know about his runaway last summer?"

"Runaway? I didn't know he ever had one. It's funny Sister Bushwell didn't tell me about it when I saw her in town at Easter."

Gogarty, she knew, delighted in driving a coach-and-four over the roughest roads in the Blue Ridge Mountains. People down there took more interest in horses than in anything else.

Martin said Gogarty had a party of visitors up from the Tidewater country. (Loudoun County people were thought to be a little jealous of the older and richer families in Tidewater Virginia.) Gogarty had wanted to give his guests a little excitement, since they made it plain that in staying with him they were tasting frontier life. He arranged to take them on a coaching party, and asked Martin to go along and sit on the box with him, whispering that he meant to make it a pretty rough trip. They set out with six passengers.

"That drive," Martin went on, "took in some of the worst roads in the mountains, Uncle Henry, and you know the best are none too good. Nobody can handle four horses better than Gogarty. We went like the wind. Up hill and down dale. The women laughed and screamed, but Hal never let on he heard them. He'd have come out all right, too, except for a funny thing. Just as we were coming down a long hill at a pretty good pace, a young deer jumped out of the bushes right in front of the horses. Of course they reared and shied. Hal kept his head, nothing got tangled. But the right front wheel smashed on a big rock beside the road. He couldn't stop the horses on the minute, so we bumped along on a dished wheel till the spokes flew out and we turned over. Then the horses went plumb crazy. Hal held on to the lines and sawed the bits, while I got forward and cut the traces. I thought I'd be kicked to death, and I did get a bad shin plaster. Our passengers were pretty well bumped up, but nobody was much hurt. One girl got her nose broken; she was a pretty girl, too. I was mighty sorry; so was Hal. It was that damn-fool deer made all the mischief. Who ever heard of a deer acting so?" Martin looked from his uncle to his aunt.

"Certainly, no one," his aunt replied with a twinkle. "It must have been got up on Hal's account. Those folks from the Tidewater do hold their heads high, though I've never seen just why they feel called upon."

The miller had laughed at the story, but he looked at his wife, not his nephew. Martin's laugh showed an upper front tooth of a bluish cast; it was set on a wooden pivot and did not fit his gum snugly. There was a story about this tooth, and the miller did not like to be reminded of it.

Martin, on his way to and from the hunts over in Clarke County, had found a pretty, homespun girl in the Blue Ridge. She used to meet him in the woods, and, as the mountain folk put it, " he fooled her." Her two brothers lay for him in the thickets along the road to give him a horsewhipping. When they jumped out from cover and caught his mare by the bit, he saw he was in for it.

" You're in the right, boys," he said amiably, " but no whip. Come at me with your fists, an' I'll do the best I can, one against two. That's fair enough."

They took him at his word, and did him in completely. They put their mark on him by knocking out one of his white teeth. (White teeth were not common in that tobacco-chewing country.) The brothers left him unconscious beside the road, but they let his horse go home to give the alarm.

Everyone in the Blue Ridge country and in Winchester knew the story of Martin's blue tooth. Many of them agreed with Sapphira : that Martin deserved what he got, but that spirited young men were wild and always would be.

Sampson's Katie, walking round and round the supper table with her flybrush, wondered what had come over her folks. " Jist a-laffin' an' a-laffin'." She was so delighted, so distracted, that more than once she let her peacock feathers dip on Miss Sapphy's high headdress. Even the Master laughed at the stories about his old neighbours; a deep laugh from the belly up, it did a body good to hear it. The Mistress's laugh was always pleasant (when she was not laughing scornfully, as a form of reprimand) : tinkling, ladylike, but with something cordially appreciative, like the occasional flash in her eyes.

Martin's laugh was just on the edge of being vulgar — rather loose, caught-in-the-act as it were. Old Washington, standing behind his mistress's chair, reflected that this was a pretty figger of a young man, but he wasn't a full-growed gen'leman yet.

Katie, excited as she was by the talk, had even keener joys in anticipation. Her eyes gloated over the good things Mr. Washington carried in to the table. She knew she would get a taste of them, though Bluebell always had the best of what went back to the kitchen. Lizzie had promised to make ice cream enough for everybody. Tap had brought squares and chunks of ice in a wheelbarrow up from the icehouse, — a dark, sawdust-filled cave under one wing of the mill. Since six o'clock old Jeff had been seated behind the laundry cabin, turning the big freezer. In winter, whenever there was a snowfall, Lizzie made "snow-cream" for the Mistress — beating the fresh, clean snow into a bowl of thick cream well flavoured with sugar and brandy. But she made ice cream only on special occasions.

The family sat so long at table that the after-supper visit in the parlour was brief that night. The Mistress admitted that she was tired.

"I seldom spend such a lively day, Martin. I had a long wait for my guest, and a very pleasant tea and supper after he got here. I like having young people with me," she added, patting his hand. She rang for Washington and told him to send Nancy upstairs to turn down Mr. Martin's bed and see that he had everything to make him comfortable.

When Martin went to his room, Nancy had already taken off the starched pillow shams and was folding up the counterpane.

"Do you like the bolster left on, sir, or jest the pillows?"

"Just the pillows. Never leave the bolster on. Take it away with you, can't you?"

"Yes indeed, sir. Is two candles enough for you? Good night, Mr. Martin."

As she was going toward the door, with the long bolster upright in her arms, Martin caught her round the shoulders and kissed her on the mouth. She let the heavy roll of feathers slide to the floor and pushed against his chest with both hands.

"Oh, please, sir, please!"

Though the candlelight was dim, he saw she was really frightened.

"Now, my girl, what's there to make a fuss about? That's the way we say good-night down where I live. You ask my aunt." She was already at the door. "Wait a minute." He pointed to the bolster lying on the carpet. "You take that thing with you, and waken me half an hour before breakfast. Don't forget."

§ III

One morning when Mrs. Blake was just about to put her bread in the oven, Nancy, with a basket on her arm, appeared at the kitchen door. Bidden to come in, she did so, rather hesitatingly.

"I jist stopped for a minute, Miz' Blake. I'm a-goin' up to the Double S. Miss Sapphy's sent me to pick some laurel for her." She spoke wanderingly and rather mournfully, Mrs. Blake noted.

"Is Mother not feeling well? She always likes to drive up the road and see the laurel herself."

"Yes, mam. Maybe she don't feel right well. You're jist puttin' your bread in, ain't you." There was no question in her voice, but sorrowful comment.

"The oven's not hot yet, but it soon will be." Mrs. Blake lifted the stove lid to put in another stick.

Nancy gasped and put out her hand beseechingly. "Oh, Miz' Blake, wait a minute, please mam do! I don't hardly know what to say, but I'm afraid to go up the holler road this mornin'."

"Afraid? What of? Blacksnakes?"

"No'm, I ain't afraid of no snakes."

Mrs. Blake dropped the stick back into the wood-box. The girl was afraid of something, sure enough. One could see it in her face, and in the shivering, irresolute way she stood there.

After covering her loaves with a white cloth, Mrs. Blake took her seat by the kitchen table. "Now sit down, Nancy, and tell me what's ailing you. Don't stand there cowerin', but sit down and speak out."

"Yes'm," meekly. "It ain't I minds goin' up there; it's jist a nice walk. Only Miss Sapphy told me to go right before Mr. Martin."

"Well, what's that got to do with it?"

"She knowed he was goin' ridin' this mornin'. He had his leggin's on."

She stopped, and Mrs. Blake waited. In a moment Nancy burst out: "Oh, Miz' Blake, he'll shorely ride up there an' overtake me in the woods!" She hid her face in her hands and began to cry. "You don't know how it is, mam. He's always a-pesterin' me, 'deed he is. I has to do his room for him, an' he's always after me. I'm 'shamed to tell you. He'll be shore to overtake me up in the woods. I lost heart when I seen you was about to bake. I thought maybe you'd walk along up with me."

" The baking can wait. I'll just check the damper and go along with you. I'd like to see that laurel myself. Now you quit crying. I'll go upstairs and slip on another dress."

Once in her own chamber, Mrs. Blake sat down to think. Her face was flushed, and her eyes blazed with indignation. She could not remember when Mrs. Colbert had not driven daily up the Hollow road to the " Double S " while the laurel was in bloom. Of course she would take her usual drive up there tomorrow, as she had done yesterday. But today she was sending Nancy. Why?

Mrs. Colbert had turned on Nancy; that was well known. Now she had the worst rake in the country staying in her house, and she was sending the girl up into the woods alone, after giving him fair warning. Did her mother really want to ruin Nancy? Could her spite go so far as that?

Rachel Blake closed her eyes and leaned her head and arms forward on her dresser top. She had known her mother to show great kindness to her servants, and, sometimes, cold cruelty. But she had never known her to do anything quite so ugly as this, if Nancy's tale were true. But there was no time to puzzle it out now. She must meet the present occasion. She quickly changed her dress and came downstairs with a basket on her arm.

"Now step along, Nancy, and brighten up. We'll go flower-picking to please ourselves."

It was still early morning; a little too warm in the sun, but wonderfully soft and pleasant in the shade. The winding country road which climbed from the post office to Timber Ridge was then, and for sixty years afterward, the most beautiful stretch in the northwestern turnpike. It was cut against gravelly hillsides bright with mica and thinly overgrown with spikes of pennyroyal, patches of rue, and small shrubs. But on the left side of the road, going west, the hillsides fell abruptly down to a mountain stream flowing clear at the bottom of a winding ravine. The country people called this the Hollow, or "Holler," road. On the far side of the creek the hills were shaded by forest trees, tall and not too thickly set: hickory and chestnut and white oak, here and there hemlocks of great height. The ground beneath them was covered with bright green moss and flat mats of wintergreen full of red berries. Out of the damp moss between the exposed tree roots, where the shade was deep, the maidenhair fern grew delicately.

The road followed the ravine, climbing all the way, until at the "Double S" it swung out in four great loops round hills of solid rock; rock which the destroying armament of modern road-building has not yet succeeded in blasting away. The four loops are now denuded and ugly, but motorists, however unwillingly, must swing round them if they go on that road at all.

In the old times, when Nancy and Mrs. Blake were alive, and for sixty years afterward, those now-naked hills were rich in verdure, the winding ravine was deep and green, the stream at the bottom flowed bright and soothingly vocal. A tramp pedlar from town, or a poor farmer, coming down on foot from his stony acres to sell a coonskin, stopped to rest here, or walked lingeringly. When the countrymen mentioned the place in speech, if it were but to say: " I'd jist got as fur as the Double e-S-S," their voices took on something slow and dreamy, as if recalling the place itself; the shade, the unstained loveliness, the pleasant feeling one had there.

Mrs. Blake and Nancy reached the curve of the first " S," and sat down on a log to rest, looking across the creek at the forest trees, which seemed even taller than they were, rising one above another on the steep hillside. There was no underbrush, except such as was prized in kings' gardens: the laurel itself. Even in those days of slow and comfortless travel, people came across the Atlantic to see the *Kalmia* in bloom; the wayward wild laurel which in June covered the wooded slopes of our mountains with drifts of rose and peach and flesh colour. And in winter, when the tall trees above were grey and leafless, the laurel thickets beneath them spread green and brilliant through the frosty woods.

"Well, Nancy," said Mrs. Blake after they had been sitting silent for a while, "we can't do better than this. The creek's narrow here, and we can easy get across on the stones."

They had not been long among the flowering bushes when Mrs. Blake heard the sharp click of horseshoes on the higher loops of the "Double S." She held up a warning finger. The hoofbeats came closer, and finally stopped. Presently there was a scraping sound of gravel and pebbles falling; the rider had found a gully where he could tie his horse.

The laurel-gatherers went on steadily about their work, bending down high branches and letting them fly back again. In a few moments young Martin crossed the creek. He must have seen two sunbonnets over there in the dark green bushes, but he doubtless thought Nancy had brought one of the coloured girls along with her.

Mrs. Blake pushed back her bonnet and confronted him with that square brow so like the miller's. Martin met the surprise admirably. His face brightened; he seemed delighted. Dropping his riding whip, he snatched off his cap.

"Why, Cousin Rachel! Have I caught you at last! Here I've been at the mill nearly two weeks, and you've never once sent word you'd like to see me. Is that the way to treat kin-folks?"

She gave him her hand, which he held longer than she liked.

"You do come to the Mill House, don't you?" he asked.

"Yes, I do. But I've been occupied. At this time of year I'm canning cherries."

"You'll let me come over and see you some night after supper? I have messages for you. I had to go to Alexandria some time back" (she knew why), "and I went on to Washington. The House was in session, and I met some of Cousin Michael's old friends. They hadn't enough good to say of him, really."

"You'd hear naught else of him," said Mrs. Blake dryly.

"Certainly not. But a man may be a fine fellow, and still not leave friends who will ask nothing better than to sit and talk about him six years after his death. Not many of us will leave friends who'll be missing us after six or seven years."

"Not many," assented Mrs. Blake. "And how

did the gentlemen come to know you were related to Mr. Blake by marriage?"

"I looked up his friends, naturally. You see, they were all so glad to have any news of you and how you were doing. They asked after you every time I saw them, and sent you a great many messages."

"Thank you. Nancy and me have got our baskets full now, and your horse is pawing on the rocks over there. We'd better be going."

"Can't I carry you home behind me? You can ride without a pillion."

"No, thank you. I partly came for the walk."

"Miss Nancy, maybe, would like to get home before her flowers wilt?" He had the brass to make this suggestion as he stooped to pick up his riding whip. "No? Then let me carry the basket to Aunt Sapphy while the flowers are fresh."

Nancy reluctantly handed him the basket. Mrs. Blake frowned, wondering why she gave in to him.

"That's a good girl!" Martin smiled at her, ran down the ravine, and crossed the creek with the basket in his hand. In a few moments they heard his horse trotting down the road.

During the homeward walk Mrs. Blake said little, but her face was flushed and grim. You could put nothing past a Colbert, she told herself bitterly. The effrontery of this scapegrace, to go to Washington and use Michael's name to introduce himself! Been to Alexandria lately! Of course he had, and everyone knew why! It was to get that blue tooth put in, to replace the one the girl's brothers had knocked out of his head on the Blue Ridge road. A doctor in Alexandria was known the country round for successful pivot work. With this ignominious brand showing every time he opened his mouth, Mart Colbert had gone to Washington and nosed about the Capitol until he found some of Michael's friends and claimed kinship. She had half a mind to tell Nancy the whole story, as a warning. But the girl was already frightened; and when she was distracted and fidgety she was likely to break things, forget orders, and exasperate her mistress.

As they parted at her gate, Mrs. Blake did say this much:

"Nancy girl, if I was you I wouldn't go into the woods or any lonesome place while Mr. Martin is here. If you have to go off somewhere, come by, and I'll go along. If I happen to be away, take Mary and Betty with you. I'll give them leave."

"Yes mam, Miz' Blake. I won't. Thank you, mam." Nancy drew her slender shoulders together as if she were cold. Some dark apprehension in her voice told more than she could say in words.

§ IV

While he was dressing next morning Martin wondered whether his ride had been spoiled by accident or by conspiracy. Had his Cousin Rachel, whom he always found a bore, gone into the woods on her own account, or had the girl entreated her company? Well, no matter. He was a match for the two of them. The only person he didn't want to offend was his Aunt Sapphy, who had urged him to visit her, and who seemed almost to be playing into his hand. As he shaved his ruddy cheeks he forgot everything except that he wanted his ham and eggs.

Mrs. Colbert was awaiting him in the dining-room. Now that Martin was here, she rose early in order to be dressed and coiffed before she joined him at breakfast. After breakfast Martin wheeled his aunt out on the porch to take the air, excused himself, and went upstairs to his room, where he expected to find Nancy making his bed. But she was not there, and the bed was still as he had left it.

Nancy was playing truant: that morning, when she came up from the miller's room, she had caught up a basket and run away to the old cherry trees behind the smokehouse. Finding no ladder handy, she went into the smokehouse to get Pappy Jeff's wooden chair. Jeff was there himself, tending the fire in a big iron kettle set deep in the earth floor. All day long, through spring and summer, the smoke from hickory chunks went up to cure and season the rows of hams and bacon hanging from the rafters of the roof.

"Pappy, kin I have your cheer to climb up a cherry tree?"

Jeff rose from his squatting position. "Sho'ly, sho'ly, honey. I don't espect no comp'ny."

But at that very moment Sampson's tall figure darkened the doorway. "See, now," Jeff chuckled, "I ain't done said no comp'ny, an' here come Sampson! Run along, chile, him an' me's got a little bizness to fix. He don't need no cheer. He kin squat on the flo', like me."

Sampson carried the chair out for her and planted it under a tree. Nancy scrambled nimbly up to the first big limb, where she could sit comfortably; could reach the cherries shining all about her and bend down the branches over her head. The morning air was still so fresh that the sunlight on her bare feet and legs was grateful. She was light-hearted this morning. She loved to pick cherries, and she loved being up in a tree. Someway no troubles followed a body up there; nothing but the foolish, dreamy, nigger side of her nature climbed the tree with her. She knew she had left half her work undone, but here nobody would find her out to scold her. The leaves over her head laughed softly in the wind; maybe they knew she had run away.

She was in no hurry to pick the cherries. She ate the ripest ones and dropped the hard ones into her basket. Presently she heard someone singing. She sat very still and gently released the branch she was holding down. He was coming from the stables, she thought.

Down by de cane-brake, close by de mill,
Dar lived a yaller gal, her name was Nancy Till.

Should she scramble down? Likely as not he would go along the path through the garden, and then he could not see her for the smokehouse. He wouldn't come prowling around back here among the weeds. But he did. He came through the wet grass straight toward the cherry trees, his straw hat in his hand, singing that old darky song.

Martin had gone to the kitchen to complain that Nancy had not done his room, and Bluebell told him Nancy was out picking cherries. There never was a finer morning for picking cherries or anything else, he was thinking, as he went out to the kitchen garden and round the stables. He didn't really intend to frighten the girl, though he owed her one for the trick she played him yesterday.

" Good morning, Nancy," he called up to her as he stood at the foot of the tree. " Cherries are ripe, eh? Do you know that song? Can you sing, like Bluebell? "

" No, sir. I can't sing. I got no singing voice."

" Neither have I, but I sing anyhow. Can't help it on a morning like this. Come now, you're going to give me something, Nancy."

His tone was coaxing, but careless. She somehow didn't feel scared of him as he stood down there, with his head thrown back. His eyes were clear this morning, and jolly. He didn't look wicked. Maybe he only meant to tease her anyhow, and she just didn't know how young men behaved over in the racing counties.

" Aren't you going to give me something on such a pretty day? Let's be friends." He held up his hand as if to help her down.

She didn't move, but she laughed a soft darky laugh and dropped a bunch of cherries down to him.

"I don't want cherries. They're sour, and I want something sweet."

"No, Mr. Martin. The sour cherries is all gone. These is blackhearts."

"Stop talking about cherries. You look awful pretty, sitting up there."

Nancy giggled nervously. Martin was smiling all the time. Maybe he was just young and foolish like, not bad.

"Who's your beau, anyhow, Nancy Till?"

"Ain't got none."

"You goin' to be a sour old maid?"

"I reckon I is."

"Now who in the world is that scarecrow, comin' on us?"

Nancy followed his eyes and looked back over her shoulder. The instant her head was turned Martin stepped lightly on the chair, caught her bare ankles, and drew her two legs about his cheeks like a frame. Nancy dropped her basket and almost fell out of the tree herself. She caught at the branch above her and clung to it.

"Oh, please get down, Mr. Martin! Do, please! Somebody'll come along, an' you'll git me into trouble."

Martin laughed. "Get you into trouble? Just this? This is nothin' but to cure toothache."

The girl had gone pale. She was frightened now, but she couldn't move, couldn't pull herself up with him holding her so hard. Everything had changed in a flash. He had changed, and she couldn't collect her wits.

"Please, Mr. Martin, please let me git down."

Martin framed his face closer and shut his eyes. "Pretty soon. — This is just nice. — Something smells sweet — like May apples." He seemed murmuring to himself, not to her, but all the time his face came closer. Her throat felt tight shut, but she knew she must scream, and she did.

"Pappy! Oh, Pappy! Come quick!"

The moment she screamed, Martin stepped down from the chair. Old Jeff came running round the end of the smokehouse, up to the foot of the tree where Nancy sat, still holding on to the limb above her. "Whassa matter, chile? Whassa matter?"

Sampson followed more deliberately, looking about him, — looking at Martin Colbert, which it was not his place to do.

Nancy said she was "took giddy like" in the tree, and was afraid she would faint and fall. Sampson got on the chair and lifted her down, but before he did so he took it in that there were already wet boot tracks on the seat. Martin, standing by, remarked that if the girl had had any sense, he would have helped her get out of the tree.

"Co'se you would, Mr. Martin," Jeff jabbered. "Young gals has dese sick spells come on 'em, an' den dey ain't got no haid. Come along, honey, you kin walk, Pappy'll he'p you."

Sampson picked up the chair and carried it back to the smokehouse. Martin strolled down the path, muttering to himself. "God, I'd rather it had been any other nigger on the place! That mill-hand don't know where he belongs. If ever he looks me in the face like that again, I'll break his head for him. The niggers here don't know their place, not one of 'em."

That afternoon Martin went for a ride. He was a trifle uncomfortable in mind. He knew he had made a blunder. He hadn't meant to do more than tease her. But after he caught her and felt against his cheeks the shiver that went over her warm flesh, he lost his head for an instant. He knew she must be pursued carelessly and taken at the right moment, off her guard. He was vexed that he had let a pleasant contact, an intoxicating fragrance, run away with him. Never mind; he would keep at a distance for a while, as if he had forgotten the cherry tree.

Riding home by the road from the post office, he spied Bluebell over yonder in the big vegetable garden. Immediately he dismounted and led his horse across the field toward her.

"Hello, Bluebell, what are you up to?"

"I'se a-pickin' lettuce fo' yo' supper, Mr. Martin." The slim black girl straightened up and stood with her bare feet wide apart between rows of lettuce.

"You don't get outdoors much, do you? I always see you in the kitchen."

"Yes, sir. I'se mos'ly heppin' Mammy." This was spoken plaintively, as if she had a hard life.

Martin laughed. He knew she was useless, except as a companion to Lizzie.

"You find time to sing, though. Aunt Sapphy's going to have you and Lizzie come into the parlour and sing for me some night. I like to hear you. Maybe I could teach you some new songs. I'm not just crazy about these hymn tunes."

Bluebell grinned. "Oh, we sings 'Home, Sweet Home,' an' 'The Gipsy's Warming.'"

Martin chuckled. "It's 'warning,' not 'warming,' my girl."

"Yes, sir. Seems jist alike when you sings it."

"Look-a-here, Bluebell, why don't they send you up to fix my room and make my bed for me? That yaller gal's no account, and solemn as a funeral. I don't like solemn girls around me."

Bluebell giggled. "Dey says how I ain't so handy wid de bedrooms. Marster, he won't let me come a-nigh his room at de mill. He *prefer* Nancy." She gave a sly suggestiveness to "prefer," lifted her eyebrows and twisted her shoulders languidly.

"He does? I can't understand that. She don't suit me." Martin patted his restive horse to quiet him. "You say she always takes care of the mill room for Uncle Henry?"

"'Deed she do. He won't have nobody else roun' him. Oh Lawdy no! I dassen' set foot in de place. Yes sir, Nancy do all de housekeepin' at de mill. Why, ev'ybody know dat. She carry down his washin' an' shine his brass mugs, an' take him bowkays. Laws, ah don' know what all she don' do at de mil-l-l."

"Damn this horse! Give me some of that green stuff to keep him still, will you?" Martin was interested.

But Bluebell took a twist of brown paper from a pocket in her very full skirt and produced a lump of crumbly brown sugar.

"Dis'll quiet him. I mos'ly carries a little to keep on han'."

Martin winked. "Comes in handy to be round the kitchen, don't it? But tell me, don't that make the other girls jealous, her going to the mill so much? Are you and Nancy good friends?"

"We gits along," languidly. "We's mos'ly friendly. Mammy don' have no patience wid her, 'cause she's stuck up, havin' white blood. When de Missus use' to favour her terribul, dat set all de culled folks agin her. But it ain't so now no mo'. Miss Sapphy turned on Nancy some while back."

"Why, what had Nancy done?"

Bluebell shrugged indifferently.

"Ah don' know. Ah don' foller nobody's do-in's. Some folks s'picions de Marster favour her now, an' de Missus don' relish her goin' down to de mill so much. Ah don' know. Ah never listens to no talk."

"That's a good rule. And you're a smart girl, Belle. Don't anybody round here call you Belle?"

"No, sah. Dey always calls me Bluebell. Dey's anoder Belle on de place; Sampson's wife, what is de haid mill-han'."

"Then I'll call you Bluebell. I certainly wouldn't call you by the name of anything be-longin' to that Sampson. Now I'm going to ask Aunt Sapphy to let you fix my room for me. The yaller gal puts on too many airs."

Martin turned and led his horse toward the hitch-post. He walked rapidly, and there was more energy in his step than common. When little Zach ran up to take his bridle, he threw him the reins without a glance, but he looked very angry, and he was talking out loud to himself. Zach caught a few words:

"By God, if I thought that old sinner had been there before me —"

The little nigger boy stared after the young man, wondering what had put him out.

Book VI

SAMPSON SPEAKS TO THE MASTER

BOOK VI

§I

Though Martin's visit proved to be a long one, his uncle saw very little of him. He never asked the young man to come down to the mill; indeed, he put his nephew out of his mind as much as possible. He realized that it meant a great deal to Sapphira to have this foolish, lively young fellow about the place. Certainly, Martin was very attentive to her; chatted with her on the porch in the morning, had tea with her in the afternoon, played cribbage with her after supper.

One night when the miller was sitting at his reading-table, he heard a knock at his door. In answer to his "Come in," Sampson appeared.

"Yes, Sampson. What is it?"

The tall mulatto stood uneasily before him. "Master Henry, I'd like to speak to you about something I got on my mind, but I don't rightly know if it's my place to."

"Speak out, Sampson."

"Mr. Henry, I'm 'fraid Mr. Martin worries Nancy a right smart."

The miller looked up and frowned. "Worries her? What do you mean? How worries her?"

"Well, sir, you know how them young fellers is. They likes to fool round a pretty girl, even if she's coloured. I don't say he means no harm, but she ain't used to them ways, an' she seems kind-a scared-like all the time. I know you wouldn't want to see harm befall her."

"Shut the door there behind you, Sampson. Now tell me: have you seen anything amiss?"

"Not rightly speaking, sir. But awhile back Nancy was pickin' cherries in one of them big trees behind the smokehouse. Me an' Jeff was in the smokehouse, an' we heard her holler like she was hurt or somethin'. We both run out an' seen Mr. Martin standin' at the foot of the tree. Before we come, he'd been standin' on the cheer Nancy took to climb up with. I seen the mud off his boots on the cheer-bottom. The gal was scared fo' sho', Mr. Henry. She was tremblin' like a leaf an' taken sick like. I took her down, an' Jeff hepped her to the cabin. I may be wrong, but I didn't like it."

The miller's face had taken on a dark flush. "I'll keep an eye on my nephew, Sampson. Sometimes a girl will make a fuss over nothing, you know."

"Yes, sir. I never seen Nancy do nothin' free nor unbecomin' when she comes an' goes."

"Nor have I. She's a good girl, and I'll look after her."

"Thank you, sir. Good night, Mr. Henry." Sampson withdrew, but his face told that he was not reassured.

The miller closed his book and began to move slowly about the room. In a flash he realized that from the first he had distrusted his nephew, though he had never thought of him in connection with Nancy. To him Nancy was scarcely more than a child. It was his habit to refer to her in that way. In reality, of course, she was a young woman. His three daughters had married when they were younger than Nancy was now. Wrath flamed up in him as he paced the floor; against his nephew and the father who begot him, against all his brothers and the Colbert blood. His own father he could hold in reverence; he was an honest man, and the woman who shared his laborious and thrifty life was a good woman. But there must have been bad blood in the Colberts back on the other side of the water, and it had come to

light in his three brothers and their sons. He
knew the family inheritance well enough. He had
his share of it. But since his marriage he had never
let it get the better of him. He had kept his marriage vows as he would keep any other contract.

The miller got very little sleep that night.
When the first blush of the early summer dawn
showed above the mountain, he rose, put on his
long white cotton milling coat, and went to bathe
in the shallow pool that always lay under the big
mill-wheel. This was his custom, after the hot,
close nights which often made sleep unrefreshing
in summer. The chill of the water, and the rays
of gold which soon touched the distant hills before
the sun appeared, restored his feeling of physical
vigour. He came back to his room, leaving wet
footprints on the floury floor behind him. Having
dressed and shaved, he put on his hat and walked
down along the mill-race toward the dam. He did
not know why, but he felt strongly disinclined to
see Nancy this morning. He did not wish to be
there when she came to the mill; it would not be
the same as yesterday. Something disturbing had
come between them since then.

For years, ever since she was a child, Nancy
had seemed to him more like an influence than a
person. She came in and out of the mill like a soft
spring breeze; a shy, devoted creature who touched

everything so lightly. Never before had anyone divined all his little whims and preferences, and been eager to gratify them. And it was for love, from dutiful affection. She had nothing to gain beyond the pleasure of seeing him pleased.

Now that he must see her as a woman, enticing to men, he shrank from seeing her at all. Something was lost out of that sweet companionship; for companionship it had been, though it was but a smile and a glance, a greeting in the fresh morning hours.

§ II

It was a little past midnight, and Sapphira had been asleep for an hour or more, when she was rudely awakened. Nancy had burst in at her door and was calling out, like someone startled.

"Yes, Miss Sapphy, here I is. Whassa matter, mam?"

"Nothing at all is the matter. Have you gone crazy, Nancy, waking me up out of my sleep like this?"

"Oh, you called out, Missy. You sho'ly did. An' I was havin' bad dreams about you."

"Be more careful what you eat, and don't come to me with your bad dreams. You know if I'm once wakened it's hard for me to get to sleep again."

"I'm dreadful sorry, Missy. I was sure I heard you callin', an' I feared you was taken bad, maybe. No, mam, I won't come in thoughtless agin. Maybe I better run down to Ma's cabin tonight, if I'm a-goin' to be res'less an' disturb you?"

"You go right back to your own bed, and control yourself properly. I won't have such crazy behaviour."

"Yes, mam." Nancy went out and closed the door softly behind her. She sat down on her pallet and wrapped a quilt about her shoulders. She did not lie down; she would wait until it was time to roll up her bed and put it in the back closet. Her rushing in upon her mistress had been a ruse. She had heard no call, but she had heard something — a cautious, barefoot step on the wide stairway which led from the upper chambers down into the open hall where she lay on her pallet before the Mistress's door. The stair treads always creaked a little; the dampness of the air kept the wood from drying thoroughly.

When the Mistress sent her back to bed, Nancy told herself that if she heard that stealthy step again, she would run down the hall and out the back door, over to her mammy's cabin. She believed someone upstairs was listening as intently as she. It was a horrible feeling. If she had the start of him, she knew she could outrun him. But then there was the curved oak banister of the stairway, smooth as glass; anybody could slide down it without making a sound. Once he was in the hall, she wouldn't have the start of him. He would be there.

At last the first grey daylight came through the wide windows at the foot of the stairs. It gave her a feeling of safety so sweet that she cuddled her head in her pillow and dozed a little. For hours the object of her terror had been fast asleep in his upstairs chamber. When he heard the sound of voices in his aunt's room, he had shrugged his shoulders and gone back to bed.

As the grey light grew stronger, Nancy rose very softly and dressed, — a simple process, since in summer she went barefoot and slept in her sleeveless " shimmy " (chemise). She had only to tie her petticoat round her waist and slip her calico dress over her head. She tiptoed down the long hall and ran out into the flower garden. The sun was just coming up over the mountain. Fleecy pink clouds were scattered about the sky, and the distant hills had turned gold. A curling mist hung over the low meadows down by the mill dam. The dew from the shrubbery was dripping in splashes upon the brick walks, and on the boxwood hedges the silvery spiderwebs trembled with glistening waterdrops. The tea roses and bleeding-hearts hung heavy, as if they would never rise again. Nobody was stirring in the negro cabins; their overgrowth of trumpet vines and gourd vines was so wet that by running into them you could take

a shower bath. It made your skin pretty, washing
your face and arms in the dew.

Oh, this was a beautiful place! Nancy didn't
believe there was a lovelier spot in the world than
this right here. She felt so joyful that her heart
beat as hard as it did last night when she was
scared. She loved everybody in those vine-covered
cabins, everybody. This morning she would be
glad to see even fat Lizzie and Bluebell. After all,
they were home folks. And down yonder was the
mill, "*and the Master so kind and so true.*" That
was in a song Miss Sapphy used to sing before she
got sick, and to Nancy those words had always
meant Mister Henry. Was it possible that she
might have lost all this happiness last night, the
night just gone? But it was still hers: the home
folks and the home place and the precious feeling
of belonging here. Maybe that fright back there
in the dark hall had been just a bad dream. Out
here it didn't seem true.

Look-a-there! the smoke was coming out of
Sampson's chimley a'ready. He was up, getting
breakfast for his children, and his wife, who managed to be sick most of the time. All the niggers
knew that Sampson not only got the breakfast: in
the small hours of the night he baked all the bread
for his family. What patience the man had! And

he never raised his low, kind voice against anybody.

One morning, soon after the above incident, the miller found his wife sitting alone at breakfast, and learned that his nephew had ridden off to Winchester for the day.

" I hope he won't use my horse too hard," he remarked. " When is he coming back? "

" Tomorrow, I think."

The miller was silent for a moment, then said with a shade of impatience, " How long is Mart going to hang around here, anyway? "

" We can't very well ask our kin how long they intend to stay with us, can we? "

" Maybe not, but he's been here about six weeks, and that's a long visit."

Sapphira smiled. " I remember my father used to tell how Benjamin Franklin said: ' *Hospitality, like fish, stinks after three days.*' That may be true in the North, but we don't feel that way in Virginia, I hope."

" Sapphira, I've had about enough of Martin's company. I never liked his father's ways, and I don't like his. What does he want here, anyway? "

" Maybe the boy wants a refuge, — from creditors."

"Or from the men of families where he's brought disgrace," her husband muttered.

She shook her finger at him. "Now, don't be too hard on him, Henry. Your brothers were all like that, you know. And Martin has a gentlemanly side which they had not. I am certainly not very lively company for a young blade to spend his evenings with, but if he is dull here he never shows it. Certainly I shall miss him when he is gone."

"Well, if you take pleasure in his company, I shan't say anything. But he will demoralize the servants. His way with the young darkies is too free. He goes into the woods across the creek to hunt mushrooms with that trifling Bluebell."

"If the servants go wrong from any visitor in the house, it's their own fault. I think they know their place better. Bluebell is a lazy, lying nigger as ever was, but I've found her smart enough to look out for herself. I doubt whether Martin would so demean himself, but it's no affair of mine." Sapphira laughed softly. It was almost as good as a play, she was thinking; the way whenever she and her husband were thinking of Nancy, they invariably talked about Bluebell.

§ III

Haying time was coming on, and now the miller turned farmer. He left the mill to Sampson and spent the mornings about the barns and stables; looking after the condition of the horses, mending the racks, seeing that Taylor cleared the haylofts of old straw and aired them for the new crop. Every year, in haying time and harvest, he gave his mill-wheels a rest. He believed the work in the open air was good for his health.

As he left the barn one morning, and was going through the negro quarters, he passed by the laundry cabin where Nancy did fine laundering for the Mistress. Hearing voices within, the girl's voice and his nephew's, he stopped short by the rain-barrel and listened.

Martin was speaking in a drawling, bantering way. "How about my fine shirts you were going to wash and iron for me, Miss Nancy Till?"

"Yes, sir. The Mistress told me to. If you'll please put 'em out in the hall for me, I'll do 'em up today."

" Now look-a-here, my girl, you just hunt in the press and find them for yourself. I don't keep account of my shirts. If you take care of my room, you look out for my washing. I ain't my own chambermaid."

The miller stepped forward and glanced in at the open door. Nancy was at the ironing-board, her eyes fixed on her work. Martin, in his riding breeches, was lounging on an old broken chair, his back against the wall and his legs stretched out in front of him. His face was turned away, but his lordly, lazy attitude and the rough familiarity of his voice were not lost upon his uncle. Colbert set his teeth and hurried through the yard down to the mill.

" Sampson," he called, " this fine weather won't last much longer, maybe. I told Taylor we would begin on the long meadow tomorrow, and you and me will go out with the men. It'll likely be a hot day, and we must get to work early, before the grass is dry. The women can turn it afterward. You'll have to go and hunt up the scythes. It's Taylor's business, but he hasn't done it. I could only find six, and there'll be eight of us in the field."

Sampson smiled reassuringly. " I 'specs I can find 'em, sir. The boys sneaks 'em away fur one thing an' another. But I'll find 'em."

Early the next morning Mrs. Blake's little girls were awakened by the ringing sound of whetstones on scythe blades. The long meadow between their house and the mill was always the first field to be cut. The mowers had assembled down by the rail fence, where the sassafras bushes screened the field from Back Creek. The miller went round the group and felt the edge of every blade. "Now, boys, I reckon we're ready to begin. Look out and keep the line straight."

The darkies scattered to their places, spat into their palms, and gripped the hand-holds. Colbert and Sampson were in the centre, and after the Master had cut the first swath the men threw themselves into the easy position of practised mowers, and the long grass began to fall. They advanced from east to west, steadily, like a good team at the plough. Colbert allowed only the seasoned mowers to work with him; the young fellows he hired out in hay-time to learn under his neighbours. As the darkies swung their scythes, they made a deep sound from the chest, the "Huh-huh" they made when they chopped wood; but they never paused except to spit into their hands.

The sun had been up several hours when the line of mowers got as far as the little iron spring which seeped up in the meadow, with a patch of tiger lilies growing round it. Here the Master beckoned the hands to come and take a drink. The water was cold and strongly flavoured with iron. The darkies passed the gourd around more than once, and stood easy; straightening their backs, and wiping their sweaty faces on shirt-sleeves already wringing wet. Every man of them kept an old hat of some sort on his head. After they had rested a few minutes, they pulled up their breeches at the waist and went back to their places. When the line moved on, the black-spotted orange lilies stood straight and tall above the fallen grass.

By and by the men began to look up anxiously at the sun: only a little spell now. They kept in line, but they certainly advanced more slowly. A cheering " Halloo " rang out across the field. The men stopped and straightened up with a grateful sigh, looking toward the Mill House stile. Yonder came young Martin, carrying in each hand a gallon jug, and behind him came Nancy and Bluebell and Nelly and Trudy and little Zach, all with baskets.

It was the custom for the mowers to have their dinner in the field. The scythes were left beside the swath last cut, and the hands gathered in the shade under a wide-spreading maple tree. In every hayfield one big tree was left for that purpose. It was always called " the mowers' tree."

After they had spread a red tablecloth on the grass and laid out the provisions, the women went away. The jugs Martin had brought were full of cold tea. The Master poured himself a full gourd, but the men drank from the jug, — it went round from mouth to mouth.

As they fell to their dinner, a pitiful figure of a negro came toward the group, not approaching directly, but circling to right and left and looking down in the grass as if he were hunting for some lost object. The darkies grinned and nudged one another. " Dar's Tansy Dave. 'Bout time he was drappin' 'long."

The Master spoke to Sampson. " Call him up, poor fellow."

In a voice that was quiet and yet carried far, the yellow man called: " Master says hurry up, Dave, or there won't be nothin' left."

The scarecrow man, bare-legged, his pants torn away to the knee, his shirt a dirty rag, approached slowly, his head hanging down. He muttered something about " been havin' a sort-a spell lately, an' didn't know as he ought-a eat nothin'."

The Master spoke up: " This is a good dinner, Dave. Set down an' eat all you want. We've got plenty."

Dave's mournful face brightened as he looked hungrily at what was spread on the red cloth. He took the chunks of corn bread and fried middling meat Sampson handed him, and drew apart from the others; just on the edge of the shade line he sat down and ate his food.

After dinner the hands lay under the tree and slept for an hour; lay on their backs, with their old hats over their faces. The miller sat leaning against the trunk and watched the ragged visitor steal across the mown field and hide himself in the sassafras bushes along the rail fence. He was thinking it was a dreary business to be responsible for other folks' lives. Time was when poor Dave, that half-witted ghost of a man, was one of the happiest boys on the place. He and Tap were the ringleaders in all the farm festivals. Dave was very clever with his mouth-organ, and he used to play for the darkies to dance on the hard-packed earth in the back yard. It was six years now since he began to go to pieces.

Six years ago a lady from Baltimore, Mrs. Morrison, had come to board with a relative three miles down the creek. She brought with her her coloured maid, Susanna, who used to come over to dance with the Colbert darkies. She was a taking wench, with big soft eyes and an irresistible giggle — light on her feet, and a pretty dancer. Colbert and Sapphira sometimes went out to watch her dance, while Dave played his mouth-organ, and the other darkies "patted" with their hands. Dave always escorted her home. Lizzie told the

Mistress that every night after supper Dave changed his shirt and went down the creek to court Susanna, and before he started he rolled over and over in the tansy bed, "to make hisself smell sweet." The nickname "Tansy Dave" had stuck to him long after he ceased to go a-courting, and after he no longer tried to make hisself smell sweet.

When Mrs. Morrison was packing to go back to the city, Dave came to Sapphira and begged her to buy Susanna, so that he could marry her. They were "promised," he said, and Susanna wanted to stay. At first his mistress laughed at him. But he cried like a little boy; threw himself on the floor and declared he "would run away and foller her if she was took off on the cars." Mrs. Colbert was melted by the boy's desperation; she told him to get up and behave himself, and she would think it over. She did think it over, and talked about it to Henry that night. Both agreed it would be foolish to buy another girl, when they had too many already. But early next morning Sapphira wakened her husband to tell him she had decided to buy Susanna if the woman would take a reasonable price for her. The girl was a good seamstress, and she could do all the fine sewing about the house.

Sapphira ordered the carriage and drove away

soon after breakfast. The miller doubted her success, but he said nothing. Susanna's mistress had once come to the Baptist church, and he did not like her arrogant manner, or the look of her. She had a small, hard face, white as flour.

When Sapphira returned, she sent down to the mill for her husband. She was greatly put out. The woman had told her at once that she thoroughly disapproved of slave-owning. When her late husband's shipping interests took him from Bath, Maine, to Baltimore, she had found it necessary to purchase two negroes for house service. In Baltimore there was no other way to get good servants. She would not sell Susanna at any price. The girl was trained for work in a town house. And after she got back to Baltimore she would never think of this crazy nigger again.

Susanna and her mistress left the neighbourhood, and Dave ran away as he had threatened. He walked to Winchester and got on the " cars." When he reached Harpers Ferry and was told he must wait there for the big train that went on to Washington, he lost heart. After a few days he came wandering home, but he was never the same boy again. He went from bad to worse; spent days, often weeks, in the mountains, wherever there was a still and moonshine whisky. Nowadays he lived in the mountains the summer through. In the fall he came down to the mill to borrow Sampson's gun and go hunting. Dave could perfectly imitate the call of the wild turkey, and he brought those wary birds home for the table; the Mistress was very fond of them. Colbert often wondered at Sapphira's forbearance with Dave. When he traded his clothes for whisky and slunk home without a shirt to his back, she would make him go wash himself in the creek, burn his rags, and put on a whole pair of pants and a new "hickory" shirt. Soon he would disappear again and not come back till winter. Taylor was pretty sure to find him in the barn some morning after the first hard freeze, buried deep in the hay. Sapphira saw that he was clothed and fed through the winter. Even Lizzie had pity on him, but she would not let him come into the kitchen to eat with the other hands. She filled a little bucket with victuals and handed it out to him.

The men finished cutting the long meadow before sundown. That night the miller excused himself early from the supper table, admitting that he was tired. He would "limber up" in a few days, he told his wife, but tonight his arms and back ached from unaccustomed exercise.

Once in his room at the mill, he threw himself upon his bed and lay still, watching the lingering twilight die. He looked forward to the next two weeks, which would take the soreness out of his back and mind. It was good for him to be out in the fields; to feel his strength drunk up by the earth and sun, and to set the pace for younger men at cutting grass and wheat.

This was a troubled time for Henry Colbert when he was alone with his thoughts. He was too often preoccupied with what Sampson had told him. Now and then the actual realization of Martin's designs would flash into his mind. The poison in the young scamp's blood seemed to stir something in his own. The Colbert in him threatened to raise its head after long hibernation. Not that he was afraid of himself. For nothing on earth, even by a glance, would he trouble that sweet confidence and affection which had been a comfort to him for so long. But it was not now the comforting thing it had been. Now he tried to avoid Nancy. Her light step on the old ax-dressed boards of the mill floor, her morning smile, did not bring the lift of spirit they used to bring.

He told himself that in trying to keep a close watch on Martin, he had begun to see through Martin's eyes. Sometimes in his sleep that preoccupation with Martin, the sense of almost being Martin, came over him like a black spell.

How was he to get rid of the fellow? In those

days, and in that country, a man could not put his
nephew out of the house unless he had flagrantly
outraged hospitality. The miller had thought seriously of trying to buy Martin off. That seemed
the likeliest possibility, though the approach would
be awkward: offering a near kinsman money to
clear out of the neighbourhood. Nevertheless he
had gone to Winchester the week before the hay
was ripe, and had drawn from the bank a larger
sum of money than he customarily kept on hand.
It was now locked in his secretary drawer. He
liked to feel that it was there, ready.

Before he undressed for the night Colbert took
from the shelf a book he often read, John Bunyan's *Holy War*, — a copy printed in Glasgow in
1763. He opened the book at a passage relating
to the state of the town of Mansoul after Diabo-
lus had entered her gates and taken up his rule
there:

> " Also things began to grow scarce in Mansoul:
> now the things that her soul lusted after were de-
> parting from her. Upon all her pleasant things
> there was a blast, and a burning instead of a
> beauty. Wrinkles now, and some shews of the
> shadow of death, were upon the inhabitants of
> Mansoul. And now, O how glad would Mansoul
> have been to enjoyed quietness and satisfaction

of mind, though joined with the meanest condition in the world."

Next he turned to the pages describing the state of Mansoul after she had been retaken and reclaimed by Prince Emmanuel, the Son of God:

"When the town of Mansoul had thus far rid themselves of their enemies, and of the troublers of their peace, a strict commandment was given out, that yet my Lord Willbewill, should search for, and do his best, to apprehend what Diabolonians were yet alive in Mansoul. . . . He also apprehended Carnal-sense, and put him in hold; but how it came about I cannot tell, but he brake prison and made his escape; yea, and the bold villain will not yet quit the town, but lurks in the Diabolonian Dens at days, and haunts like a Ghost, honest men's houses at nights."

In this book he found consolation. An honest man, who had suffered much, was speaking to him of things about which he could not unbosom himself to anyone.

Book VII

NANCY'S FLIGHT

BOOK VII

§ I

The wheat harvest was nearly over. Nancy and her companions had been carrying dinner to the mowers, in the big wheat field on the other side of Back Creek. On her way home Nancy slipped from the company and ran through Mrs. Blake's yard to her kitchen door. Mary and Betty had finished washing the dishes, and their mother was preparing to roast coffee beans in the oven. After one look at Nancy's face, she told the children they could go down the road and watch Grandfather cutting his wheat. When they were gone, she turned to the yellow girl.

"What's the matter now, child? Has that scamp been pestering you again? Set down and tell me."

Nancy dropped into a chair. "Oh, I'm most drove out-a my mind, I cain't bear it no longer, 'deed I cain't! I gets no rest night nor day. I'm goin' to throw myself into the millpawnd, I am!" She bowed her head on her arms and broke into sobs.

"Hush, hush! Don't talk so, Nancy, it's wicked. Stop your crying, and tell me about it." She stood over the girl, stroking her quivering shoulders until the sobs grew more throaty and, as it were, dried up. Nancy lifted her face.

"Miz' Blake, you's the only one I got to talk to. He's just after me night an' day, till I wisht I'd never been bawn."

"I guess a good many of us wish that, sometimes. But we come right again, and bear our lot. Have you said anything to my father?"

"How could I, Miz' Blake? I'd die a' shame to speak it before that good ole man. I got nobody I kin come to but you."

"Then you must try to make it plain to me, Nancy. Can't you keep out of his way?"

"It's worst at night, Miz' Blake. You know I sleeps outside Miss Sapphy's door, an' he's right over me, at the top of the stairs. One night I heard him comin' down the stairs in his bare feet, an' I jumped up an' run into the Mistress's room, makin' out I thought I heered her callin' me. She was right cross 'cause I'd waked her up, and sent me back to my bed, an' I layed there awake till mornin'. If I was to sleep sound, he could slip in to me any time. If I hollered, the Mistress would put it all on me; she'd say I done somethin' to make him think I was a bad girl. Another time I heard him slippin' down at night, an' I jumped an' run to old Mr. Washington. You know he sleeps on a cot in the wine closet. He give me his bed, an' he set up all night in the hall. So I cain't run in to the Mistress agin, an' I hates to go to Mr. Washington. He needs his rest. Why, Miz' Blake, there ain't no stoppin' Mr. Martin. He kin jist slip into my bed any night if I happens to fall asleep. I got nobody to call to. I cain't do nothin'!"

Here Nancy sprang from her chair and stood with her hands pressed against her forehead and her blue-black hair.

"I tell you, I'd druther drown myself before he got at me than after! Only I want *somebody* as'll speak up for me to the Master, an' tell him I didn't do it from wickedness. Please, mam, tell him how I was drove to it."

When she spoke of the Master, she began to cry again, and could not go on.

Presently Mrs. Blake said quietly but resolutely: "I'm a-going to get you away from all this, Nancy.

Mind you, no more talk about the mill dam. You're young and have life before you. I've seen how things were going, and I've been figuring on how to get you away from the mill. You've not been real happy over there for a good while back."

"No'm, not since she turned on me." Nancy spoke absently, as if talking to herself. "It ain't nothing she *does* to me. I don' know what it is, but she never looks at me no more. She's jist turned on me."

Mrs. Blake took her by the shoulders, as if to rouse her. "Now you must listen to me, Nancy. Would you be brave enough to go away from here to a better place, where you'd be safe? I can't run Mart Colbert out of the neighbourhood, but I think I can get you away. Would you go?"

"I'd go anywheres to git away from him. I'd sooner go down to Georgia an' pick cotton, 'deed I would."

"It won't come to that, Nancy. Just you hold out a little longer, and I'll get you out of these troubles. Have you said anything to Till?"

Nancy looked up at her with wondering, startled eyes. "To Maw? How could I, mam?"

Mrs. Blake turned away and began to put slow wood in her stove to get on with her roasting. "Here come my girls up the road. You better let them go along home with you. Maybe Mother's missed you, but if they're with you, nothing will be said."

After Nancy and the children were gone, Mrs. Blake sat down to watch over the pans of browning coffee. She understood why Nancy did not go to Till for advice and protection. Till had been a Dodderidge before ever she was Nancy's mother. In Till's mind, her first duty was to her mistress. Ever since Mrs. Colbert had become an invalid, Till's position in the house was all-important; and position was dear to her. Long ago Matchem had taught her to "value her place," and that became her rule of life. Anything that made trouble between her and the Mistress would wreck the order of the household.

Nancy had come into the world by accident; the other relation, that with the Dodderidges, Till regarded as one of the fixed conditions you were born into. Beginning with Jezebel, her kin had lived under the roof and protection of that family for four generations. It was their natural place in the world.

Yes, Mrs. Blake knew why Till shut her eyes to what was going on over at the Mill House. And she realized once more that she herself was by nature incapable of understanding her mother. Ever since she could remember, she had seen her mother show shades of kindness and cruelty which

seemed to her purely whimsical. At this moment
Mrs. Blake could not for the life of her say
whether Mrs. Colbert had invited this scapegrace
to her house with the deliberate purpose of bringing harm to Nancy, or whether she had asked him
merely for the sake of his company, and was now
ready to tolerate anything that might amuse him
and thus prolong his stay. This was quite possible,
since Mrs. Colbert, though often generous, was
entirely self-centred and thought of other people
only in their relation to herself. She was born that
way, and had been brought up that way.

Yet one must admit inconsistencies. There was
her singular indulgence with Tansy Dave, her real
affection for Till and old Jezebel, her patience
with Sampson's lazy wife. Even now, from her
chair, she took some part in all the celebrations
that darkies love. She liked to see them happy.
On Christmas morning she sat in the long hall and
had all the men on the place come in to get their
presents and their Christmas drink. She served
each man a strong toddy in one of the big glass
tumblers that had been her father's. When Tap,
the mill boy, smacked his lips and said: " Miss
Sapphy, if my mammy's titty had a-tasted like
that, I never would a-got weaned," she laughed as
if she had never heard the old joke before.

When the darkies were sick, she doctored them,

sent linen for the new babies and had them brought for her to see as soon as the mother was up and about. Recalling these things and trying to be fair to her mother, Mrs. Blake suddenly rose from her chair and said aloud:

"No, it ain't put on; she believes in it, and they believe in it. But it ain't right."

§ II

By the next morning's stage Mrs. Bywaters sent an important letter to David Fairhead, asking him to come out to Back Creek as soon as possible. He rode up to her gate next evening on his old grey horse. That night Mrs. Blake and Mr. Whitford, the carpenter, met at the post office to confer with him. When they were seated in the postmistress's private parlour, where they would not be disturbed, Mrs. Blake revealed her bold purpose. Mrs. Bywaters sat by to encourage her.

To the two women the plan seemed a desperate undertaking. No negro slave had ever run away from Back Creek, or from Hayfield, or Round Hill, or even from Winchester. But Mr. Fairhead was reassuring. He told them the underground railroad was now busier than ever before. The severe Fugitive Slave Law, passed six years ago, had by no means prevented slaves from running away. Its very injustice had created new sympathizers for fugitives, and opened new avenues

of escape. From as far away as Louisiana, negroes were now reaching Canada; the railroads
and the lake steamboats helped them. If a negro
once got into Pennsylvania or Ohio, he seldom
failed to go through.

Fairhead explained to Mrs. Blake how simple
it would be to get Nancy from Winchester to
Martinsburg, and from there into Pennsylvania.
While she sat by, he wrote a letter to his cousin in
Martinsburg, who would be very glad to assist
her. This letter would go off by the stage tomorrow morning.

Mr. Whitford said he could manage for Mrs.
Blake as far as Winchester. He had a light can-
vas-covered spring-wagon in which he carried coffins to distant burying-grounds. Chairs for two
women could be put inside under the canvas, and
they could make the drive to town unseen by anyone. Travelling late at night, they would reach
Winchester in good time to take the morning
stage for Martinsburg.

Mrs. Blake went home greatly reassured. But
the hardest thing to arrange, the interview she
most dreaded, was still before her.

The following night she set out for the mill by
the creek road, where she would scarcely be likely
to meet any of the house servants. Once at the
mill, she went to the north window of her father's

room. He was within, sitting at his table; not reading, but gazing moodily at the floor.

" Can I come in, Father? " she asked quietly.

" Is that you, Rachel? Wait a minute." He came out to the platform where the wagons were unloaded, took her hand, and led her through the dark passage to his room. When he closed the door he shot the bolt.

Mrs. Blake sat down and drew a long breath. " Well, Father, I've come over to have a talk with you. I blame myself I didn't come before this. I reckon you know what it's about."

She looked to him for recognition, but he sat frowning at the floor. It tried her that he gave her no encouragement, when he certainly must know what was on her mind. She was tired, and the road round by the creek had seemed long.

" Father," she broke out indignantly, " are you going to stand by and see a good girl brought to ruin without lifting a finger? "

The miller crossed the room and shut down the open window. His face had flushed red, and so had Mrs. Blake's. She went on with some heat.

" You surely know that rake Mart Colbert is after Nancy day and night. He'll have her, in the end. She's a good girl, but the Colbert men never let anything get away. He'll catch her somewhere, and force her."

Her father clenched his two powerful fists. "No he won't! It's only by the mercy of God I haven't strangled the life out of him before now."

"Then why don't you do something to save her?"

He made no reply. His daughter sat watching him in astonishment. His darkly flushed face, his clenched hands gave her no clue to what was going on in his mind; struggle of some sort, certainly. She had always known him quick to act, had never seen him like this before.

"I may be overstepping my duty," she said at last, "but I couldn't sit with my hands folded and see what's going on here. She's come to me for help, and I couldn't hold back. I'm a-going to get Nancy away from here and on the road to freedom."

He looked up now, and met her eyes with a flash in his own. "If only it were possible, Rachel—"

"Well, it is possible. Mr. Fairhead's offered to help me. It ain't so hard as it seems to us out here. Slaves are running away in plenty now. He's got Quaker friends that will get the girl into Pennsylvania. About five miles out of Martinsburg there's a ferry will take me and Nancy across the Potomac. When we get across, a conveyance will meet us and carry her on from house to house. In a day and a night I can get her into safe hands."

"And then what's to become of her?"

"The Quakers will get her somehow over into New York State an' put her on the cars. There's a railroad runs right up through Vermont into Canada, out-a reach of slave-catchers. He says the railroad men are glad to help. It's a-going on all the time now. They hide runaway slaves in the baggage cars an' take 'em clear through to Montreal."

"Montreal? Now what would a young girl like her do in a big strange city? An' they talk nothing but French up there, I've heard. You must be gone crazy, Rachel. There she'd come to harm, for certain. A pretty girl like her, she'd be enticed into one of them houses, like as not." The miller wiped his forehead with his big handkerchief. The closed room was getting very hot.

"Father, I can tell you there's many folks in big cities that are a sight kinder than some folks on this farm. You know Mother bears a hard hand on Nancy, and has for a good while back. How the girl's stood it, I don't know. God forgive me, but it looks to me like she'd brought that scamp here a-purpose, an' she's tried right along to throw the girl in his way. She knows Nancy lays unprotected out in the open hall every night, where he can sneak down to her. He's tried it more'n once, an' the pore thing had to run in to old Washington in the wine closet, an' he let her have his cot. Another time, — "

The miller sprang to his feet, knocking over the chair behind him. "Hush, Rachel, not another word! You and me can't talk about such things. It ain't right. What do you come telling this to me for, if you've fixed it up with Mr. Fairhead and Whitford? I can't be a party to make away with your mother's property."

"I come to you because we need money, a hundred dollars, to get her safe through into Canada. An' I ain't got it. If I had, I'd turn to nobody."

Henry Colbert walked slowly about the room, his eyes downcast. He was ashamed to show such irresolution before his daughter. She would think he grudged the money, maybe. The money was there, in his secretary. It made her plan possible, made it almost an accomplished fact; a loss that could never be made up to him. He had been humouring himself with the hope that, once Martin was out of the way, things might be as they used to be. But every word his daughter said made him know Nancy could never be the same again, could never be happy here. He must face it.

"Rachel," he said presently in his natural voice, "nothing must pass between you and me on this matter; neither words nor aught else. Tomorrow night I will go to bed early, and I will leave my coat hanging on a chair by the open window here — " he raised the north window and propped it up on its stick. " Now I will walk home with you."

" No, Father, thank you. We might meet somebody. I'd sooner we weren't seen together to-night."

The following night Mrs. Blake came again to the mill by the creek road. Her father's room was dark, but the window was open. She put in her hand, took out the coat that hung on the chair-back, and felt through the pockets. From the inside pocket she took a flat package of bank-notes.

The miller, in his bed, heard her come and go. He lay still and prayed earnestly, for his daughter and for Nancy. *Not a sparrow falleth to the ground without Thy knowledge.* He would never again hear that light footstep outside his door. She would go up out of Egypt to a better land. Maybe she would be like the morning star, this child; the last star of night. . . . She was to go out from the dark lethargy of the cared-for and irresponsible; to make her own way in this world where nobody is altogether free, and the best that can happen to you is to walk your own way and be responsible to God only. Sapphira's darkies were better cared for, better fed and better clothed, than the poor whites in the mountains. Yet what ragged, shag-haired, squirrel-shooting mountain man would change places with Sampson, his trusted head miller?

§ III

Mr. Whitford was to be at Mrs. Blake's house at one o'clock in the morning. Starting at that hour, he would be unlikely to meet travellers on the road, and he would get into Winchester well before daylight. He and his passengers were to have an early breakfast with the old Quaker who was a friend of the miller and of Mr. Fairhead. From the Quaker's house they would take the stage for Martinsburg. If Mrs. Blake chanced to meet an acquaintance on the street or in the stage, it was quite natural that she should be going to Martinsburg on a visit, attended by her mother's maid.

Nancy was to come over to Mrs. Blake's about midnight. When all was still at the Mill House, she got up from her pallet, dressed in the dark, and slipped out of the back door, carrying her shoes and stockings in one hand, and in the other an old pillowcase stuffed with her spare clothes and her few belongings.

When she got to the stile, she sat down behind it and put on her shoes. It was the dark of the moon, and anyone crossing the meadow could not easily be recognized. But if she met anyone, the fact that she was wearing her winter shawl and a hat would arouse curiosity. To travel as Mrs. Blake's lady's maid, she must be dressed for town. Her hat was an old black turban of Mrs. Colbert's. Till had put a red feather on it when Nancy accompanied her mistress to Winchester at Easter.

Mrs. Blake was sitting on her doorstep, waiting, and her house was dark. She drew a sigh of relief when she saw a figure come out of the meadow and cross the road. She met Nancy at the gate, took her into the parlour, pulled down the blinds, and lighted a candle.

"Now, Nancy, here's my old carpet sack. I'm going to give it to you for your own, and you can pack away in it whatever you've got in your bundle there. From now on we must look spruce, like we was going visiting. I'm glad you've got a feather in your hat. It's real becoming to you, and it was a good hat in the first place, when Mother got it. I see you've brought along one of the old reticules. That will be handy to carry the letters I've written out for you to show to the Quaker folks, and maybe to the railroad men, telling how you're a deserving girl and I stand behind you. But when

I give you your money, in Martinsburg, you must put it in your stockings. Never let it off your body."

"Oh, Miz' Blake, the reticule ain't mine! Miss Sapphy give it to me yisterday, with three pairs a-her good silk stockings for me to darn. I did mean to darn 'em today, but some way I jist couldn't git down to it. I been kind-a flighty in the haid like. I'll mend 'em as soon as I git there, an' send 'em back by stage, or somehow." Nancy was nervously packing the carpetbag as she spoke.

Mrs. Blake glanced up, and then stepped quickly into the kitchen to get command of herself. She thought how vague, even to her, was this "there" that Nancy spoke of — *there* was Canada, wasn't it? Mrs. Blake herself had never been farther north than Baltimore. She had always thought of Boston as very, very far north. And Montreal was away, away longer off than Boston. And Nancy spoke of sending things back by stage! For a moment she felt her courage sink.

When she returned to the parlour, she set about straightening the tidies on the chairs, speaking over her shoulder in a matter-of-fact tone. "You better leave your darning right here. I'll mend 'em up neatly and send 'em over. Things often get lost on the stage. Listen! There's Mr. Whitford for sure. He's stopped his horses at our gate. I'll get my things on."

A few minutes later Mrs. Blake walked out of her door in her Sunday best, even to black gloves, and Nancy walked behind her, carrying the carpet sack. Mr. Whitford helped them into the back of his wagon and then untied his horses. Very soon the team splashed through Back Creek. Mrs. Blake had a moment of apprehension and glanced at Nancy. But the girl seemed worn out and dulled by the day's excitement; her head drooped forward on her knees as if she were dozing. It was not until they were passing the old Elliot place, and a jolt over a limestone ledge threw her chair to one side, that she wakened up.

The houses along the road were all dark. The first lighted windows were in the disreputable tavern near Hoag Creek, a place where bad men got together: moonshiners and sheep-stealers and fist-fighters who wore brass knuckles in a fight, drank bad whisky, and threw dice and told dirty stories about decent folk until daybreak. The sound of horses' hoofs on the road at this late hour brought the revellers reeling and shouting out into the road.

"Hold on, stranger, give us a ride up the Gap! Who be ye? Issa damned Gov'ment officer! Pull him in an' fill him up, fellers. He's after moon-shiners, an' we'll show him some."

"We'll give him a whole bellyful-a moon-shine!"

Bill Hooker, who had only one eye and bragged he had never cut his hair, caught the horses by the bits, but they kicked at him, and he fell in the road.

"Drag him out," Whitford called, "and go back where you came from. I'm Whitford, of Back Creek, and I'm carrying a coffin home."

The rowdies let out a spiritless yell or two, and stumbled back toward the tavern.

"Hope you wasn't scared, Mrs. Blake," said Whitford. "It's funny; those fellows don't blink an eye at murder, but they don't like to interfere with a corpse."

§ IV

In Martinsburg Mr. Taverner, Mr. Fairhead's cousin, met the stage and took Mrs. Blake and her companion to his house, where his wife made them very comfortable.

After dark he drove the two women out to the ferry in his buggy. He had warned the ferryman that he would be sending two friends across to-night, so the ferryman asked no questions. He said " Good evening, mam," to Mrs. Blake, and held out his hand to help her into the boat. Nancy followed. She had never been in a boat before, never seen any stream wider than Back Creek.

The Potomac ran strong here, leaped over ledges and boulders with a roaring sound like a waterfall. It was cold out on the river, and the churned water threw up a light spray. Nancy's winter shawl was not heavy enough to keep out the chill; Mrs. Blake could feel her shivering as they sat on the narrow seat. The boat swayed and swung on its wire, however carefully the ferryman used his oars to right it. Once Mrs. Blake thought they certainly had broken loose. When they reached shallow water, the ferryman tied up his boat and helped the two women to climb up the rocks to level ground. He called: "Hello," but there was no answer.

"We got a little cabin here, where passengers waits. Their folks is sometimes late comin'. You better come in an' set down on the bench till your folks come. Don't be skeered of nothin'; I'll be around. Mr. Taverner told me one of the passengers was to go back. I'll be right around where you kin call me."

Mrs. Blake and Nancy sat huddled together in the damp little hut which smelled of tobacco smoke and rotting wood. A cricket was chirping sharply inside, and outside was the perpetual, agitating rush of the river, — a beautiful sound when you are not frightened, but Nancy was. And Mrs. Blake was disappointed. So far, the journey had been swift and pleasant, but this halt was a little disturbing. She could feel the courage oozing out of the girl beside her. It might be best to say something, something practical, to divert Nancy's thoughts. She asked her to feel whether her garters were tied tight, and her money safe in her stockings. In a flash she knew she had said the wrong thing. The girl wilted altogether.

"Oh, Miz' Blake, please mam, take me home!

I can't go off amongst strangers. It's too hard.
Let me go back an' try to do better. I don't mind
Miss Sapphy scoldin'. Why, she brought me up,
an' now she's sick an' sufferin'. Look at her pore
feet. I ought-a borne it better. Miz' Blake, please
mam, I want to go home to the mill an' my own
folks."

"Now don't talk foolish. What about Martin?"

"I kin keep out-a his way, Miz' Blake. He
won't be there always. I can't bear it to belong
nowheres!"

"You've been a brave girl right along, an' you
mustn't fail me now. I took a big risk to get you
this far. If we went back, Mother would never
forgive you — nor me. It would be worse than
before. These Quaker folks will be kind to you,
an' you'll be bright an' happy, like you used to be.
If you ain't happy when you get to your journey's
end, I'll fetch you back somehow. Don't give way,
after all Mr. Fairhead and Mr. Whitford have
done for you. Remember, you were ready to throw
yourself in the mill dam."

"Yes'm," the girl breathed. But Mrs. Blake
didn't believe she had heard her at all. She
couldn't take anything in; her mind was frozen
with homesickness and dread. After that they sat
in silence.

The nerve-racking suspense did not go on much longer. Through the rushing of the river Mrs. Blake thought she heard the rattle of wheels and hoofs over a stony road.

"Listen, I believe they're coming now. Listen!" She hurried out of the cabin, dragging Nancy after her.

An old chaise emerged from the dark wood, and the driver got out. He was a coloured man, she knew at once from his voice; a negro preacher, as it proved, and a freed man. In greeting Mrs. Blake he took off an old beaver hat, which he wore as the sign of his calling.

"Is this Miz' Blake? I'm 'fraid I kep' you waitin', mam. I had some trouble on de way. De road, from Williamsport on, is very bad, an' they's been heavy rains. De folks sent me along to drive, 'cause Reverend Fairhead wrote how de gal was young an' easy skeered. I am a minister of de gospel, well known hereabouts, an' dey figgered she wouldn't feel so strange wid me."

"I'm glad you came, Uncle. The girl's lost heart a little. She's never been away from home before, an' she's afraid with strangers."

The tall black man turned to Nancy and put a hand on her shoulder. "Dey ain't strangers, where you're goin', honey. Dey calls theyselves Friends, an' dey is friends to all God's people.

You'll be treated like dey had raised you up from a chile, an' you'll be passed along on yo' way from one kind fambly to de next. Dey got a letter all 'bout you from de Reverend Fairhead, an' dey all feels 'quainted. We must be goin' now, chile. We want to git over the line into Pennsylvany as early tomorrer as we kin." There was something solemn yet comforting in his voice, like the voice of prophecy. When he gave Nancy his hand, she climbed into the chaise. He put her bag in after her, then turned to Mrs. Blake, still holding his hat over his chest.

"An' you, lady, the Lawd will sho'ly bless you, fo' He said Hisself: Blessed is the merciful."

He untied his team and waited a moment, but Nancy never said a word; not to him, not to Mrs. Blake. She had stood dumb all the while the old man spoke to her, as if she were drugged; indeed she was, by the bitterest of all drugs. The preacher clucked to his horses, seeing that the girl had no word of farewell to say. But as they started off, Mrs. Blake called out to her:

"Good-bye, Nancy! We shall meet again."

Book VIII

THE DARK AUTUMN

BOOK VIII

§ I

Mrs. Bywaters's youngest son walked into Mrs. Blake's yard one morning with a letter. She was sitting in her parlour by an open window, sewing. He took off his cap and went to speak to her through the window:

"Good day, Mrs. Blake. I brought a letter for you. Mother said it must have been slipped into the letter-box late last night, for she didn't find it till she was stamping the mail for the stage this morning. She thought it might be important, so she sent me down with it."

"Thank you, Jonathan. That was real thoughtful of your mother."

After Jonathan went away, Mrs. Blake sat contemplating the envelope he had brought. It was addressed in her mother's neat handwriting. She had heard nothing from the Mill Farm since her return from Winchester by stage three days ago — except from Bluebell. That spineless darky girl (doubtless sent by Lizzie) had come across the meadow after dark and guilelessly asked Mrs. Blake if she had seen nothin' of Nancy lately. Nobody at home had seen her, an' they was a-gittin' right worried. Taylor he thought they ought to drag the mill dam, but Trudy said maybe she was a-stayin' over to Miz Blake's, or was some'ers Miz Blake knowed about.

No, Mrs. Blake knew nothing of Nancy's whereabouts, and Bluebell had better run along home, as Mrs. Blake was going to a prayer meeting at the church.

"Yes'm. I's a-goin'. We cain't find out nothin' at home, 'cause Miss Sapphy ain't once spoke Nancy's name since we foun' her bed empty one mawnin'. An' Till ain't spoke her name, nuther. When Maw axed her where was Nancy, she jist tole her to mind her business. But we 'speck Till had some talk wid de Missus, 'cause right from the fust day Till's been doin' Master's room an' Mr. Martin's. Seem like Till don't miss her gal much. Las' night when Taylor axed her mus' he drag de mill dam, she tole him he could do what he pleased, an' not to come pesterin' her."

Mrs. Blake resolutely put on her bonnet and pointed to the kitchen door. When Bluebell went out, she shut it behind her and drew the bolt. This was the only word she had had from the mill people.

The letter Jonathan had brought was doubtless something final, since it bore a stamp and came through the post office. People on Back Creek did not send letters to their neighbours through the post. A note to be sent up or down the road was not even put into an envelope. It was folded, turned down at one corner, and carried to the addressee by one of the boys or girls about the place. Government stamps were considered an extravagance. At last Mrs. Blake opened the letter and read:

> *Mistress Blake is kindly requested to make no further visits at the Mill House.*
> *Sapphira Dodderidge Colbert*

Well, that was best, Mrs. Blake agreed, as she folded up the paper. Her mother would meet this situation with dignity, as she had met other misfortunes. She would not set the slave-catchers on to track Nancy. She would not question anyone. She knew, of course, that the girl could never have got away without help, and this letter told that she understood who had contrived her escape. The Colbert darkies must know that Mrs. Blake's house had been closed for two days, and that Mary and Betty stayed with Mrs. Bywaters while their mother was away. She was sorriest for the hurt this would be to her mother's pride. Nancy's disappearance would be the talk of the neighbourhood. Every time Mrs. Colbert drove out she would meet inquiring faces. The whisperings and surmises among her own servants would be a trial to her. Mrs. Blake knew how her mother hated to be overreached or outwitted, and she was sorry to have brought another humiliation to one who had already lost so much: her activity on horse and foot, her fine figure and rosy complexion.

The property loss Mrs. Colbert would bear lightly. Tansy Dave was certainly a property loss, and she had never complained or tried to punish him. But if he had actually run away and stayed in Baltimore, his mistress would likely enough have had him seized and brought back.

A girl like Nancy, refined and very pretty, skilful with her needle and in chamber work, would easily fetch a thousand dollars, maybe more. But Mrs. Blake did her mother the justice to believe that this money out was not the thing that cut to the quick. She unfolded the letter again, and as she looked at it, tears rose slowly to her eyes.

"It's hard for a body to know what to do, sometimes," she murmured to herself. "I hate to mortify her. Maybe I ought to a-thought about how much she suffers, and her poor feet, like Nancy said to me that night in the dark cabin by that roaring river. Maybe I ought to have thought and waited."

All through the month of August Mrs. Blake was busy sewing for her girls, to get them ready for school. She saw no one from the Mill House except her father, who walked home with her from church every Sunday. Nancy's name was never mentioned between them.

One Sunday morning fat Lizzie caught Mrs. Blake outside the church door and came at her. "Howdy, Miz Blake. Now maybe you knows when Nancy is comin' home? I axed Miss Sapphy only yiste'day, an' she says to me she s'posed Nancy'd come back from Ches'nut Hill when she was sent fur. Now Tap come up wid a nigger from Ches'nut Hill in Winchester, an' he tells Tap dey ain't never seen sight a' Nancy down dar. It begins to look like Taylor's right, an' she drownded herse'f in de dam. He says dat's all a pack a' lies 'bout dem risin' to de top in fo' days. She might easy a-ketched on a big root an' be down dar still."

By this time a dozen eager listeners had

gathered round, and Mrs. Blake gave Lizzie a dark look. "Here comes your master. You had better ask him."

Lizzie turned and saw the miller coming up the path. With a "God a'mighty!" she hurried into the church and up the narrow stairs to the gallery as fast as a woman of her figure could go.

After the first October frosts, when everyone went into the woods to gather chestnuts and hickory nuts, Mrs. Blake and her two little girls happened to come upon a nutting party from the Mill House. Till was among them. She met Mrs. Blake with such warmth as she seldom betrayed and called her by her given name.

"It's surely nice to lay eyes on you agin, Miss Rachel. It does me good to see you lookin' fine and hearty."

Mrs. Blake asked after her mother's health.

"I'm right worried about her, Miss Rachel. Doctor Clavenger comes out from Winchester every week to see her. Sometimes he draws the water off, an' then she's easier. She don't git up for breakfast no more. She stays in bed all day till I dresses her an' takes her into the parlour for tea."

Their talk was suddenly interrupted by shouts and scrambling. Tap, the nimblest of the mill boys, had climbed a tall chestnut tree and was

thrashing the branches with a pole. The little
darkies shouted as the nuts showered down, and
all the women fell on their knees and began scratch-
ing among the dried leaves and stuffing the nuts
into their bags and baskets. Till and Mrs. Blake
picked side by side, and once when they were
bending over close together, Till asked in a low,
cautious murmur: "You ain't heard nothin', Miss
Rachel?"

"Not yet. When I do hear, I'll let you know.
I saw her into good hands, Till. I don't doubt
she's in Canada by this time, amongst English
people."

"Thank you, mam, Miss Rachel. I can't say
no more. I don't want them niggers to see me
cryin'. If she's up there with the English folks,
she'll have some chance."

§ II

No one on Back Creek could remember a finer autumn; frosts before sunrise, summer heat at noon, chill nights. All morning the mountain lay in a soft blue haze, and in the afternoon broad fans of heavy golden sunlight warmed its back and flanks. The colour on the hillsides, in the low meadows, and along the streams had never been more brilliant. Little rain fell in October, and the trees held their leaves. The great maples in Mrs. Blake's yard were like blazing torches; scarlet leaves fluttered softly down to the green turf, leaving the boughs above still densely covered.

With November the weather changed. Heavy rains set in. There was scarcely a clear day. The earth was soon soaked, the meadows became boggy, and all the streams rose. Back Creek overflowed its low banks and rushed yellow and foaming into the mill road. The schoolroom under the Baptist Church, set deep in the hillside, became very damp. Suddenly David Fairhead's school was closed; nearly half his pupils were in bed with ulcerated throats or diphtheria.

It was a rare winter when there was not an outbreak of diphtheria in Hayfield or Back Creek or Timber Ridge. This year it came before winter began. Doctor Brush rode with his saddle-bags all day long from house to house, never bothering to wash his hands when he came or went. His treatment was to scour throats with a mixture of sulphur and molasses, and to forbid his patients both food and water. If he found " white spots," he declared the case diphtheria, and the patient was starved until the spots were gone. Few children survived his treatment.

Late one evening in the week after the school had been closed, Mr. Whitford was driving his covered spring-wagon along the big road, carrying two coffins up to Timber Ridge. As he passed Mrs. Blake's house he saw that her front door stood wide open, and a flickering light came from the parlour windows. This was a signal to passers-by that help of some sort was needed within. As he slowed his team, Mrs. Blake herself ran out into the road to hail him.

" We're in trouble here, Mr. Whitford. Both my girls are sick, and I want you to carry word to the post office. Yes sir, they've been ailing with colds since yesterday, but tonight, just after supper, they were taken very bad. Maybe Mrs. Bywaters can come down to help me. And maybe she can send one of her boys along with you to hunt for the doctor. He's likely somewhere on the ridge. I daren't leave the house, and not a soul has come along the road till you."

" I'll get somebody here in no time, Mrs. Blake. Don't you worry, mam." Mr. Whitford whipped up his horses.

At the post office there was a brief consultation between Mrs. Bywaters and David Fairhead. Most people, though not all, believed that diphtheria was " catching." Clearly the postmistress, who had to be on duty and see people every day, should not go where there was a contagious disease. Fairhead said he would go: Whitford could carry him back to Mrs. Blake's, then drive up to Timber Ridge, deliver his coffins, and trail Doctor Brush until he found him.

When Fairhead reached Mrs. Blake's house, he found her in an upstairs bedroom, holding the wash-basin for Betty, who was nauseated. After she laid the child back on her pillow, she rose and said: " Oh, I'm glad it's you, David." She fronted him with a strange, dark look which frightened him. He was very fond of these children. He stood still and tried to think. Mrs. Blake had got the girls into their nightgowns, braided their hair, and put them into two cots in the room they shared together. Fairhead told her he felt sure they ought not to be in the same room.

"There's the spare room, across the hall, David. The bed's made up. You can carry Mary over and put her in it."

Toward morning Mr. Whitford brought word that Doctor Brush would stop at Mrs. Blake's about sun-up, if she would have a good breakfast and plenty of coffee ready for him. The doctor came, looked down the girls' throats, found his "white spots," and seated himself in the dining-room to enjoy his breakfast. Immediately David Fairhead started for the mill.

The miller was standing before his little looking-glass, in the act of shaving, when Fairhead called to him through the open window.

"Mr. Colbert, I've come from Mrs. Blake's house. Both her little girls are sick with bad throats. Doctor Brush is over there now. I thought you might like to talk to him before he leaves."

The miller put down his razor, caught up his coat, and set off with David across the meadow. When he came home an hour later, he went directly to his wife's room and sat down beside her.

"Sapphira, I was called over to Rachel's. The trouble has reached her house. Both the girls are down with it."

She rose on her pillows and gave him a searching look. "You mean it's diphtheria?"

"That's what Brush says."

"Brush! Why, the man's a complete ignoramus! It may be measles, for all he knows. Have you sent to town for my doctor?"

"No. I've only just got back from Rachel's. I thought I'd better consult you. It's come so sudden I've hardly had time to realize it."

"But why haven't you sent for Clavenger?" She reached under her pillow for the bell and rang it vigorously. Old Washington answered.

"Washington, send somebody down to the mill for Tap. This minute, as fast as you can get him here. Now, Henry, you must start Tap off for Winchester on your own horse. Who has Rachel got over there to help her?"

"David Fairhead left Mrs. Bywaters's in the middle of the night and went down. He is going to stay with them. He's a better nurse than any of the women around here."

His wife scarcely heard him. "There comes Tap. Call him in here. I want to talk to him, and you see to saddling Victor."

Tap came to the chamber door, which the Master had left ajar, and called softly through the crack: "You wants to see me, Miss Sapphy?"

"Yes, I do. Come in."

The boy came in, holding a rag of a hat in his two hands. The darky men never went about the place without some sort of hat on their heads.

"Now, Tap, listen to me," she began sternly. Tap stood rigid; he opened his eyes, prepared for a scolding. "I'm sending you to town to get Doctor Clavenger. My two granddaughters are very sick."

The black boy stared at her, his shoulders went slack. "Not Miz Blake's li'l gals, mam?" he asked wistfully.

"Yes, Mary and Betty have diphtheria, and you must go and get Doctor Clavenger here as quick as you can. You can ride faster than Mr. Henry or Sampson, because you are lighter. I can't write to Doctor Clavenger, my hand is too bad" (she held it up), "so you must explain to the doctor that children are dying around here every day, and I will never forgive him if he don't get out to us before night. You understand this is serious, Tap?"

Tap squeezed his crumpled hat tighter to his chest. "You kin depen' on me, Miss Sapphy. I'll git de doctah, I'll fetch 'im back. You kin depen' on me." His naturally lively voice had sunk to something deep and shadowy. He slipped out of the room, and only a few minutes later his mistress saw him flash down the driveway on Victor, the fast trotter.

Word of why Tap was going to town had got through the house, and Till came unbidden to Mrs. Colbert. She stood at the foot of the bed in her usual correct attitude, her hands under her white apron.

"Kin I do anything, Miss Sapphy?"

"Yes, Till, you can. I want you to go over to Mrs. Blake's and see how things are. Mr. Henry has been over, but men don't notice very close. And you take one of the boys along, to carry a bundle of clean sheets and pillowcases. Rachel can't have many ahead, because she's always giving them away. While you're there, look around sharp for what's needed. Don't ask Rachel, but just see for yourself. And if you're not afraid, slip in and peep at the children, and tell me how they look."

"It ain't likely I'd be afraid, Missy. Who must I tell to wait in, if you rings your bell?"

Mrs. Colbert gave a dry, sad little laugh: "Well, there isn't anybody *but* you, now, Till. You might ask Washington and Trudy to sit outside in the hall."

§ III

Tap came back from Winchester, but he came alone. Doctor Clavenger had been called to Berryville to do a critical operation which the local doctor dared not undertake. Mrs. Clavenger, his wife, sent a letter to Mrs. Colbert, promising that as soon as her husband got home he would mount a fresh horse and start for Back Creek. She thought, indeed she felt sure, that he would be there by midday tomorrow. To the miller and Fairhead, who were awaiting him at Mrs. Blake's, tomorrow seemed a long way off.

It was heart-breaking to see the children suffer, and to hear them beg for water. Their grandfather could not bear it. He went home, and digging down into the sawdust of the icehouse under his mill, he found some lumps of last year's ice. It was going soft, maybe a little wormy, but he brought it over and let the girls hold bits of it in their mouths. He was not afraid of Doctor Brush, and he had authority as the head of his family. The ice helped them through the long afternoon.

Fairhead insisted on sitting up with the patients that night. Mrs. Blake would relieve him at four o'clock in the morning. The two had an early supper together in the kitchen. As Mrs. Blake went up the back stairs, she called down: " I've made a chicken broth for you, David, and left it there on the table to cool. Put some hickory sticks in the stove to hold the fire, and you can warm it up any time in the night you feel the need of it."

Fairhead went out into the yard to get the cool air into his lungs. Sick-rooms were kept tightly closed in those days. The blue evening was dying into dusk, and silvery stars were coming out faintly over the pines on the hill. Fairhead was deeply discouraged. He believed Doctor Clavenger would know just what to do; but tomorrow might be too late.

Clavenger was everything that poor old Brush was not: intelligent, devoted to his profession — and a gentleman. He had come to practise in Frederick County by accident. While he was on the staff of a hospital in Baltimore, he fell in love with a Winchester girl who was visiting in the city. After he found that she would never consent to live anywhere but in her native town, he gave up the promise of a fine city practice and settled in Winchester. A foolish thing to do, but Clavenger was like that.

While Fairhead was walking up and down the yard, he kept an eye on the windows of Mrs. Blake's upstairs bedroom. As soon as the candle-light shone there, it would be time for him to go to his patients. He circled the house, picked up some sticks from the wood-pile, and was about to go into the kitchen when he saw through the window something which startled him. A white figure emerged from the stairway and drifted across the indoor duskiness of the room. It was Mary, bare-foot, in her nightgown, as if she were walking in her sleep. She reached the table, sank down on a wooden chair, and lifted the bowl of broth in her two hands. (She must have smelled the hot soup up in her bedroom; the stair door had been left open.) She drank slowly, resting her elbows on the table. Streaks of firelight from the stove flick-ered over her and over the whitewashed walls and ceiling. Fairhead knew he ought to go in and take the soup from her. But he was unable to move or to make a sound. There was something solemn in what he saw through the window, like a Communion service.

After the girl had vanished up the stairway, he still stood outside, looking into the empty room, wondering at himself. He remembered how some-times in dreams a trivial thing took on a mysteri-ous significance one could not explain. He might have thought he had been dreaming now, except that, when at last he went inside, he found his soup bowl empty.

Fairhead climbed the stairs slowly and went to Betty's room. After he had washed out her throat with a clumsy thing called a swab, he got the last morsel of ice (wrapped in sacking on the window sill) and put it in her mouth. She looked up at him gratefully and tried to smile. He whispered that he would soon come back to her, took the candle, and crossed the hall to Mary's room. He did not know what he might find there. He listened at the crack of the door; dead silence. Shading the light with his hand, he went in softly and approached the bed. Mary was lying on her side, fast asleep. Last night she had not slept at all, but tossed and begged for water. Her mother, who had sat up with her, said she was delirious and had to be held down in bed. Fairhead leaned over her; yes, the evil smell was on her breath, but anyhow he was not going to waken her to wash her throat. He went back to Betty, who liked to have him turn her pillow and sit near her.

Mary slept all night. When Mrs. Blake came in at four in the morning and held her candle before the girl's face, she knew that she was better.

Doctor Clavenger rode up to the hitch-block about noon. He had dismounted and tied his horse before Fairhead could cross the yard to greet him. The doctor looked as fresh as if he had not been without sleep for more than thirty hours. He said the ride out had rested him, adding: "It's beautiful country." There was even a flush of colour in his swarthy cheeks, and as he shook hands he gave David a warm, friendly look from his hazel eyes, which in some lights were frankly green.

"I am glad to find you here, David. You will be a great help to me, as you were when Doctor Sollers had pleurisy. Now, in the first place, can you get word to the mill and ask Mr. Colbert to send over a fresh horse for me? I am hoping he can take my mare to his stable and rest her overnight. I will ride her back to town tomorrow."

"Yes, sir. Till is in the kitchen. She will carry the message."

"Good." He took the young man's arm and walked slowly toward the house. At the front door he stopped, turned round, and stood looking back at the blue slopes of the North Mountain. "How much better the line of the mountain is from here than from Mrs. Colbert's yard!" He traced the long backbone of the ridge in the air with his finger. After taking a deep breath, he went inside.

When he greeted Mrs. Blake in the hallway, he

asked very courteously for a pitcher of fresh water and two glasses; his ride, he said, had made him thirsty. David dropped the saddle-bags he was carrying and ran out to the springhouse for cold water. Doctor Clavenger thanked him and drank with evident gratification. Then he delicately waved Mrs. Blake to the stairway and followed her, carrying the pitcher and the two glasses, which she supposed were to be used for medicines. But the first thing he did was to lift Mary on his arm and hold a glass one-third full to her lips. She swallowed it eagerly and easily. He laid her down, crossed the hall, and did the same for Betty. When she choked and gurgled, he said soothingly: "That's very good. Some of it went down; enough for this time."

Mrs. Blake and Fairhead both stood by while he examined his patients, but he asked few questions of them. He was deliberate and at ease. He looked at the children, even at their throats, very much as he had looked at the mountain — sympathetically, almost admiringly, David thought. If Mrs. Blake spoke up to give him information about the course of their illness, he raised his hand in gentle rebuke. He talked to the children, however, while he was working over them, talked soothingly, as if he had come to make things pleasant for them. Even when they saw the swabs coming, they felt no dread. His swabs were very different from Dr. Brush's, and he did not use sulphur and molasses. He stayed with them nearly two hours, and as he left he blew a kiss to each with: "Be good girls for me, until I come tomorrow."

When he went downstairs, he gave Mrs. Blake and Fairhead clear and positive instructions, saying in conclusion:

"Leave the windows open as I put them, Mrs. Blake. This is a fine day at last, — let the air and sunlight into their rooms. They will not take cold, but if you are afraid of that, put more blankets over them. And tell your father he must try to find more bits of ice in that cave of his, for the little girls."

Fairhead went with the doctor to the hitch-post, where the miller's horse stood in readiness. "Doctor Clavenger, could you spare me a moment? There's something I think I ought to tell you."

The doctor sat down on the lower step of the hitch-block, leaned back against the second step, and relaxed into a position of ease, as if he meant to spend the afternoon there looking at the mountain. When David began to tell him what he had seen in the kitchen last night, he listened attentively, with his peculiar expression of thinking directly behind his eyes. He did not once interrupt, but when David ended with: " and I can't believe she is any the worse for it," the doctor gave him a quizzical smile.

"We'd best keep this a secret between ourselves, here on Back Creek. The child was hungry. Your warm broth satisfied that craving, and she went to sleep. Her system began to take up what it needed. That's very simple. What surprises me is that you were struck dumb outside the window and did not go blundering in and take the child's chance away from her." The doctor stepped up on the block (he was a short man) and swung his leg over the saddle.

Late the next afternoon Mrs. Colbert was sitting by the parlour fire, her chair turned so that she could look out of the north windows. Since midsummer she had, without comment, changed her habit of life. Now she did not leave her bed until tea-time. She was watching the meadow path, anxiously awaiting her husband's return. He had been over at Rachel's since morning, and Doctor Clavenger, she knew, had come out soon after midday. She could not understand why some word of how he found the children had not been sent her.

At last she saw the miller coming across the meadow. She shook her head and sighed. His slow gait, the slackness of his shoulders, told her that he brought no good news. As he came through the yard he did not look up or glance toward the windows. She heard him open and close the front door, but he did not come in to her at once. When he came he did not speak, but stood by her chair, stooping down to warm his hands at the fire.

"Poor Rachel," he brought out at last, "little Betty has gone."

"Oh, Henry! Couldn't Clavenger do anything?"

"I reckon not. It was so sudden. It happened while he was there. I was in Mary's room, and all at once he came to the door and lifted his finger, looking at me sharp. I went back with him, and in a minute she was gone; just slipped away without a struggle, like she was dropping asleep. At first we couldn't believe it."

"And Mary?"

"She is better. Clavenger says she will get well. We must be thankful. But Betty was my little dear."

Mrs. Colbert reached out and caught his hand. "I know, Henry. I know. But these things are beyond us. One shall be left and the other taken. It's beyond us." She was silent for a moment. Suddenly she gripped his cold fingers and broke

out with something of her old masterfulness:
"And, Henry, Mary will get *so much more* out
of life!"

"More for herself, maybe," the miller sighed.
"But I doubt if she will be as much comfort to
others. The gentle spirit has left us."

"Sit down, dear. Get my old hassock yonder
and sit low, close to the fire. Your hands are like
ice. This is a time when we must both think."
She reached under the tea-table for the red flask
and poured the rum into her empty teacup. He
drank it obediently. She knew he was too tired to
talk, so they sat in silence. When Washington
came in for the tray, she put her finger to her lips
and pointed to the hot-water jug. He understood
that meant fresh tea for the Master. In a few
moments he brought it, and left without making
a sound. Supper was ready, but he saw this was no
time to speak of it.

All this while the Mistress was thinking, turning things over in her mind. She had not seen
Rachel since Nancy's disappearance, months ago.
She was wondering how far she could count upon
herself. At last, when she had quite made up
her mind, she put her hand on her husband's
drooping shoulder.

"Henry, it will be hard for Rachel and Mary
over in that house now. Everything will remind

them. Why not ask them to come here and spend
the winter with us? I would like to have them, on
my own account. I'm not as able as I was last
year. Rachel is very proud, but I expect if you told
her I have failed, and we ought to have someone
here, she would come. Mary would be nice company for me. I miss the child when I don't see her.
And if anything was to happen to me, the place
wouldn't run down and be so lonesome like for
you. Till is a good housekeeper, but the other
darkies wouldn't mind her one week if there wasn't
a woman of the family to stand behind her. You'd
soon have bedlam here. Rachel and Till together
would keep things up as they ought to be."

Colbert felt a chill run through him. Sapphira
had never before spoken to him of the possibility
that something might happen to her this winter.
Though now she mentioned this very casually, it
struck terror to his heart. He seemed in a moment
to feel sharply so many things he had grown used
to and taken for granted: her long illness, with all
its discomforts, and the intrepid courage with
which she had faced the inevitable. He reached
out for her two hands and buried his face in her
palms. She felt his tears wet on her skin. For a
long while he crouched thus, leaning against her
chair, his head on her knee.

He had never understood his wife very well, but

he had always been proud of her. When she was young, she was fearless and independent, she held her head high and made this Mill House a place where town folks liked to come. After she was old and ill, she never lowered her flag; not even now, when she knew the end was not far off. He had seen strong men quail and whimper at the approach of death. He, himself, dreaded it. But as he leaned against her chair with his face hidden, he knew how it would be with her; she would make her death easy for everyone, because she would meet it with that composure which he had sometimes called heartlessness, but which now seemed to him strength. As long as she was conscious, she would be mistress of the situation and of herself.

After this long silence, in which he seemed to know that she followed his thoughts, he lifted his head, still holding fast to her hands, and spoke falteringly. "Yes, dear wife, do let us have Rachel here. You are a kind woman to think of it. You are good to a great many folks, Sapphy."

"Not so good as Rachel, with her basket!" She turned it off lightly, tweaking his ear.

"There are different ways of being good to folks," the miller held out stubbornly, as if this idea had just come to him and he was not to be teased into letting go of it. "Sometimes keeping people in their place is being good to them."

" Perhaps. We would all do better if we had our lives to live over again." She was silent for a moment, then added thoughtfully: " Take it all in all, though, we have had many happy years here, and we both love the place. Neither of us would be easy anywhere else."

Book IX

NANCY'S RETURN

(Epilogue — Twenty-five years later)

BOOK IX

§ I

Twenty-five years had passed since Mrs. Blake took her mother's slave girl across the Potomac. The Civil War, which came on so soon after Nancy ran away, was long gone by when Back Creek folks saw the yellow girl again.

In all that time the country between Romney and Winchester had changed very little. The same families were living on their old places. There were new people at the Colbert mill, of course, and several new brick houses with ambitious porticoes now stood on the turnpike between Winchester and Timber Ridge. But the wooden foot-bridge over Back Creek hung just as it did in the Colberts' time, a curious " suspension " bridge, without piles, swung from the far-reaching

white limb of a great sycamore that grew on the
bank and leaned over the stream. Mrs. Bywaters,
though now an old woman, was still the postmistress. She had not been removed in the " carpetbag " period, when so many questionable Government appointments were made. During the
war years, when Federal troops were marching up
and down the valley, her well-known Northern
sympathies stood the Confederate soldiers in good
stead. When they were home on leave, they could
always hide from search parties in her rambling
garrets. Her house was exempt from search.

The war made few enmities in the country neigh-
bourhoods. When Willie Gordon, a Rebel boy
from Hayfield, was wounded in the Battle of Bull
Run, it was Mr. Cartmell, Mrs. Bywaters's father,
who went after him in his hay-wagon, got through
the Federal lines, and brought him home. While
the boy lay dying from gangrene in a shattered leg
(Doctor Brush never attempted an amputation,
and Doctor Clavenger was far away on Lee's
staff), the Hayfield people, regardless of political
differences, came in relays, night and day, and did
the only thing that relieved his pain a little : they
carried cold water from the springhouse and with
a tin cup poured it steadily over his leg for hours
at a time.

Mr. Whitford's son enlisted in the Northern

army, as his father's son might be expected to do. His nearest neighbour, Mr. Jeffers, had a son in Ashby's cavalry. The fathers remained friends, worked their bordering fields, and talked to each other across the rail fence as they had always done. Both men admired young Turner Ashby of Fauquier County, who held the Confederate line from Berkeley Springs to Harpers Ferry, — so near home that word of his brilliant cavalry exploits came out to Back Creek with the stage-driver. The war news from distant places came slowly, sometimes long after the event, but Stonewall Jackson and Ashby, both operating in Frederick County, gave people plenty to talk about.

Ashby fell in the second year of the war, shot through the heart after his horse had been killed under him, leading a victorious charge near Harrisonburg, on the sixth day of June. Even today, if you should be motoring through Winchester on the sixth of June, and should stop to see the Confederate cemetery, you would probably find fresh flowers on Ashby's grave. He was all that the old-time Virginians admired: *Like Paris handsome and like Hector brave.* And he died young. "Shortlived and glorious," the old Virginians used to say.

After Lee's surrender, the country boys from Back Creek and Timber Ridge came home to their farms and set to work to reclaim their neglected fields. The land was still there, but few horses were left to work it with. In the movement of troops to and fro between Romney and Winchester, all the livestock had been carried away. Even the cocks and hens had been snapped up by the foragers.

The Rebel soldiers who came back were tired, discouraged, but not humiliated or embittered by failure. The country people accepted the defeat of the Confederacy with dignity, as they accepted death when it came to their families. Defeat was not new to those men. Almost every season brought defeat of some kind to the farming people. Their cornfields, planted by hand and cultivated with the hoe, were beaten down by hail, or the wheat was burned up by drouth, or cholera broke out among the pigs. The soil was none too fertile, and the methods of farming were not very good.

The Back Creek boys were glad to be at home again; to see the sun come up over one familiar hill and go down over another. Now they could mend the barn roof where it leaked, help the old woman with her garden, and keep the wood-pile high. They had gone out to fight for their home State, had done their best, and now it was over.

They still wore their army overcoats in winter, because they had no others, and they worked the fields in whatever rags were left of their uniforms. The day of Confederate reunions and veterans' dinners was then far distant.

When Nancy came back after so many years, though the outward scene was little changed, she came back to a different world. The young men of 1856 were beginning to grow grey, and the children who went to David Fairhead's basement school were now married and had children of their own.

This new generation was gayer and more carefree than their forbears, perhaps because they had fewer traditions to live up to. The war had done away with many of the old distinctions. The young couples were poor and extravagant and jolly. They were much given to picnics and campmeetings in summer, sleighing parties and dancing parties in the winter. Every ambitious young farmer kept a smart buggy and a double carriage, but these were used for Sunday church-going and trips to Winchester and Capon Springs. The saddle-horse was still the usual means of getting about the neighbourhood. The women made social calls, went to the post office and the dressmaker, on horseback. A handsome woman (or a pretty girl) on a fine horse was a charming figure to meet on the road; the close-fitting riding-habit with long skirt, the little hat with the long plume. Cavalry veterans rose in the stirrup to salute her as she flashed by.

§ II

It was a brilliant, windy March day; all the bare hills were still pale fawn colour, and high above them puffy white clouds went racing like lambs let out to pasture in the spring. I was something over five years old, and was kept in bed on that memorable day because I had a cold. I was in my mother's bedroom, in the third storey of a big old brick house entered by a white portico with fluted columns. Propped on high pillows, I could see the clouds drive across the bright, cold blue sky, throwing rapid shadows on the steep hillsides. The slats of the green window shutters rattled, the limp cordage of the great willow trees in the yard was whipped and tossed furiously by the wind. It was the last day I would have chosen to stay indoors.

I had been put into my mother's bed so that I could watch the turnpike, then a macadam road with a blue limestone facing. It ran very near us, between the little creek at the foot of our long front yard and the base of the high hills which shut the winter sun from us early.

It was a weary wait for the stage that morning. Usually we could hear the rattle of the iron-tired wheels and the click of the four shod horses before they came round the curve where the flint mile-stone with deep-cut letters said: ROMNEY — 35 MILES. But today there was a high wind from the west. Maybe we could not hear the stage coming, Mrs. Blake remarked to Aunt Till.

For I was not alone in the room. Two others were there to keep me company. Mrs. Blake sat with her hands lying at rest in her lap. She looked almost as if she were in church. Aunt Till was sitting beside her; a spare, neat little old darky, bent at the shoulders but still holding herself straight from the hips. The two conversed very little; they were waiting and watching, just as I was. Occasionally my mother came in, going with her quick, energetic step to the window and peering out. She was young, and she had not the patience of the two old women.

"Don't get excited," she would say to me. "It may be a long while before the stage comes."

Even my father was awaiting the stage. He had not gone out to cut timber with the men to-day, but had sent them into the woods with Moses, son of the Colberts' old Taylor, as the boss. Father was down in his basement tool-room under the portico steps, tinkering at something. Probably he was making yellow leather shoes for the front paws of his favourite shepherd dog — she wore out so many, racing up and down the stony hillsides in performing her duties.

There was as much restlessness inside the house as there was outside in the wind and clouds and trees, for today Nancy was coming home from Montreal, and she would ride out from Winchester on the stage. She had been gone now for twenty-five years.

Ever since I could remember anything, I had heard about Nancy. My mother used to sing me to sleep with:

Down by de cane-brake, close by de mill,
Dar lived a yaller gal, her name was Nancy Till.

I never doubted the song was made about our Nancy. I knew she had long been housekeeper for a rich family away up in Canada, where it was so cold, Till said, if you threw a tin-cupful of water into the air, it came down ice. Nancy sometimes wrote to her mother, and always sent her fifty dollars at Christmas.

Suddenly my mother hurried into the room. Without a word she wrapped me in a blanket, carried me to the curved lounge by the window, and put me down on the high head-rest, where I could look out. There it came, the stage, with a trunk on top, and the sixteen hoofs trotting briskly round the curve where the milestone was.

Mrs. Blake and Aunt Till had followed my mother and now stood behind us. We saw my father running down the front yard. The stage stopped at the rustic bridge which crossed our little creek. The steps at the back were let down, my father reached up to hand someone out. A woman in a long black coat and black turban alighted. She carried a hand-satchel; her trunk was to go to Till's cabin on the old mill place. They crossed the bridge and came up the brick walk between the boxwood hedges. Then I was put back into bed, and Mrs. Blake and Till returned to their chairs. The actual scene of the meeting had been arranged for my benefit. When I cried because I was not allowed to go downstairs and see Nancy enter the house, Aunt Till had said: "Never mind, honey. You stay right here, and I'll stay right here. Nancy'll come up, and you'll see her as soon as I do." Mrs. Blake stayed with us. My mother went down to give Nancy the hand of welcome.

I heard them talking on the stairs and in the hall; my parents' voices excited and cordial, and another voice, low and pleasant, but not exactly "hearty," it seemed to me, — not enough so for the occasion.

Till had already risen; when the stranger followed my mother into the room, she took a few uncertain steps forward. She fell meekly into the arms of a tall, gold-skinned woman, who drew the little old darky to her breast and held her there, bending her face down over the head scantily covered with grey wool. Neither spoke a word. There was something Scriptural in that meeting, like the pictures in our old Bible.

After those few moments of tender silence, the visitor released Aunt Till with a gentle stroke over her bent shoulders, and turned to Mrs. Blake. Tears were shining in the deep creases on either side of Mrs. Blake's nose. "Well, Nancy, child, you've made us right proud of you," she said. Then, for the first time, I saw Nancy's lovely smile. "I never forget who it was took me across the river that night, Mrs. Blake."

When Nancy laid aside her long black coat, I saw with astonishment that it was lined with grey fur, from top to toe! We had no coats like that on Back Creek. She took off her turban and brushed back a strand of her shiny, blue-black hair. She wore a black silk dress. A gold watch-chain was looped about her neck and came down to her belt, where the watch was tucked away in a little pocket.

"Now we must sit down and talk," said my mother. That was what one always said to visitors. While they talked, I looked and listened. Nancy had always been described to me as young, gold-coloured, and "lissome"— that was my father's word.

" Down by de cane-brake, close by de mill, Dar lived a yaller gal — " That was the picture I had carried in my mind. The stranger who came to realize that image was forty-four years old. But though she was no longer lissome, she was other things. She had, I vaguely felt, presence. And there was a charm about her voice, though her speech was different from ours on Back Creek. Her words seemed to me too precise, rather cutting in their unfailing distinctness. Whereas Mrs. Blake used to ask me if she should read to me from my "hist'ry book" (*Peter Parley's Universal*), Nancy spoke of the his-to-ry of Canada. I didn't like that pronunciation. Even my father said "hist'ry." Wasn't that the right and easy way to say it? Nancy put into many words syllables I had never heard sounded in them before. That repelled me. It didn't seem a friendly way to talk.

Her speech I counted against her. But I liked the way she sat in her chair, the shade of deference in her voice when she addressed my mother, and I liked to see her move about, — there was something so smooth and measured in her movements. I noticed it when she went to get her handbag, and opened it on the foot of my bed, to show us the pictures of her husband and three children. She spoke of her mistress as Madam, and her master as Colonel Kenwood. The family were in England for the spring, and that was why Nancy was able to come home and visit her mother. She could stay exactly six weeks; then she must go back to Montreal to get the house ready for the return of the family. Her husband was the Kenwoods' gardener. He was half Scotch and half Indian.

Nancy was to be at our house for the midday dinner. Then she would walk home with her mother, to stay with her in the old cabin of her childhood. The " new miller," as he was still called, though he had now been running the mill for some seventeen years, was a kind man from over the Blue Ridge. He let Till stay on in her cabin behind the Mill House, work her own garden patch, and even keep a pig or two.

When my mother and father and Mrs. Blake went down to dinner, Nancy and Till sat where they were, hand in hand, and went on talking as if I were not there at all. Nancy was telling her mother about her husband and children, how they had a cottage to themselves at the end of the park, and how the work was divided between the men and the maids.

Suddenly Till interrupted her, looking up into her face with idolatrous pride.

"Nancy, darlin', you talks just like Mrs. Matchem, down at Chestnut Hill! I loves to hear you."

Presently they were called downstairs to the second table, to eat the same dinner as the family, served by the same maid (black Moses' Sally). My mother gave me an egg-nog to quiet me and pulled down the blinds. I was tired out with excitement and went to sleep.

During her stay on Back Creek Nancy came often with her mother to our house. She used to bring a small carpetbag, with her sewing and a fresh apron, and insisted upon helping Mrs. Blake and Moses' Sally in whatever housework was under way. She begged to be allowed to roast the coffee. "The smell of it is sweeter than roses to me, Mrs. Blake," she said laughing. "Up there the coffee is always poor, so I've learned to drink tea. As soon as it's browned, I'll grind a little and make us all a cup, by your leave."

Our kitchen was almost as large as a modern music-room, and to me it was the pleasantest room in the house, — the most interesting. The parlour was a bit stiff when it was not full of company, but here everything was easy. Besides the eight-hole range, there was a great fireplace with a crane. In winter a roaring fire was kept up in it at night, after the range fire went out. All the indoor and outdoor servants sat round the kitchen fireplace and cracked nuts and told stories until they went to bed.

We had three kitchen tables: one for kneading bread, another for making cakes and pastry, and a third with a zinc top, for dismembering fowls and rabbits and stuffing turkeys. The tall cupboards stored sugar and spices and groceries; our farm wagons brought supplies out from Winchester in large quantities. Behind the doors of a very special corner cupboard stood all the jars of brandied fruit, and glass jars of ginger and orange peel soaking in whisky. Canned vegetables, and the preserved fruits not put down in alcohol, were kept in a very cold cellar: a stream ran through it, actually!

Till and Nancy usually came for dinner, and after the dishes were washed they sat down with Mrs. Blake in the wooden rocking-chairs by the west window where the sunlight poured in. They took out their sewing or knitting from the carpet-bag, and while the pound cake or the marble cake was baking in a slow oven, they talked about old times. I was allowed to sit with them and sew patchwork. Sometimes their talk was puzzling,

but I soon learned that it was best never to interrupt with questions, — it seemed to break the
spell. Nancy wanted to know what had happened
during the war, and what had become of everybody, — and so did I.

While she sat drawing her crochet hook in and
out, she would say: " And what ever did become
of Lizzie and Bluebell after Miss Sapphy died?"

Then Till would speak up: " Why, ain't I told
you how Mr. Henry freed 'em right after Missy
died, when he freed all the niggers? But it was
hard to git rid of free niggers befo' the war. He
surely had a sight a' trouble gittin' shet of them
two! Even after he'd got Lizzie a good place at
the Taylor House hotel in Winchester, they kep'
makin' excuse to stay on, hangin' 'round the
kitchen. In the end he had to drive 'em into town
himself an' put 'em down at the hotel, an' tole 'em
fur the las' time they wasn't needed at the mill
place no more. You know he never did like them
two niggers. He took a wonderful lot a' trouble
gittin' good places fur his people. You remembers
Sampson, honey?"

" Why, of course I do, Mother. He was Master's steadiest man." At this moment Till would
likely be on her feet in a twinkle with: " Before I
begin on Sampson, I'll just turn the bread fur you,
Mrs. Blake. I seem to smell it's about ready."

When all the pans had been changed about, Till would sit down and continue:

"Well, Mr. Henry got Sampson a wonderful good place up in Pennsylvany, in some new kind of mill they calls roller mills. He's done well, has Sampson, an' his childern has turned out well, they say. Soon as the war was over, Sampson come back here, just to see the old place. The new miller treated him real clever, and let him sleep in old Master's mill room — he don't use it only like a kind of office, to see folks. Sampson come to my cabin every day he was here, to eat my light bread. 'Don't never trouble yourself to cook me no fancy victuals, Till,' he'd say. 'Just give me greens an' a little fat pork, an' plenty of your light bread. I ain't had no real bread since I went away.' He told me how in the big mill where he works the grindin' is all done by steam, and the machines runs so fast an' gits so hot, an' burns all the taste out-a the flour. 'They is no real bread but what's made out-a water-ground flour,' he says to me."

"And Tap, whatever became of him, Mrs. Blake?"

Then followed a sad story. I knew it well. Many a time I had heard about Tap, the jolly mill boy with shining eyes and shining teeth, whom everybody liked. "Poor Tap" he was always called now. People said he hadn't been able to stand his freedom. He went to town (" town " always meaning Winchester), where every day was like circus day to a country-bred boy, and picked up various jobs until the war was over. Early in the Reconstruction time a low German from Pennsylvania opened a saloon and pool hall in Winchester, a dive where negroes were allowed to play, and gambling went on. One night after Tap had been drinking too much, he struck another darky on the head with a billiard cue and killed him. The Back Creek farmers who remembered Tap as a boy went to his trial and testified to his good character. But he was hanged, all the same. Mrs. Blake and Till always said it was a Yankee jury that hanged him; a Southern jury would have known there was no real bad in Tap.

Once Nancy looked at Mrs. Blake with a smile and asked her what had become of Martin Colbert. I had never heard of him. Mrs. Blake glanced at her in a way that meant it was a forbidden subject. " He was killed in the war," she said briefly. " He'd got to be a captain in the cavalry, and the Colberts made a great to-do about him after he was dead, and put up a monument. But I reckon the neighbourhood was relieved."

More than anything else, Nancy wanted to

know about the last days of her old master and mistress. That story I could almost have told her myself, I had heard about them so often. Henry Colbert survived his wife for five years. He saw the beginning of the Civil War, and confidently expected to see the end of it. But he met his death in the haying season of 1863, when he was working in the fields with the few negroes who begged to stay on at the Mill Farm after the miller had freed all his wife's slaves. The Master was on top of the hayrack, catching the hay as Taylor forked it up to him. He stepped backward too near the edge of the load and fell to the ground, striking his head on a limestone ledge. He was unconscious when the field-hands carried him into the house, and he died a few hours later.

When my parents went for a long horseback ride, they sometimes took me as far as Till's cabin, and picked me up again on their way home. It was there I heard the old stories and saw Till's keepsakes and treasures. They were stowed away in a pinewood chest with a sloping top. She had some of the miller's books, the woolly green shawl he had worn as an overcoat, some of Miss Sapphy's lace caps and fichus, and odd bits of finery such as velvet slippers with buckles. Her chief treasure was a brooch, set in pale gold, and under the crystal was a lock of Mr. Henry's black hair and Miss Sapphy's brown hair, at the time of their marriage. The miller himself had given it to her, she said.

In summer Till used to take me across the meadow to the Colbert graveyard, to put flowers on the graves. Each time she talked to me about the people buried there, she was sure to remember something she had not happened to tell me before. Her stories about the Master and Mistress were never mere repetitions, but grew more and more into a complete picture of those two persons. She loved to talk of Mrs. Colbert's last days; of the reconciliation between the Mistress and Mrs. Blake that winter after Betty died, when Mrs. Blake and Mary stayed at the Mill House. The Mistress knew she had not long to live. The tappings had become more frequent; Doctor Clavenger came out from Winchester twice a week now. He told Till he had never known anyone with that kind of dropsy to live so long as Mrs. Colbert; he said it was because her heart was so strong. But the day would come when the pressure of the fluid would be too heavy, and then her heart would stop.

" She kept her bed most all day that last winter," Till would go over it, " an' she liked to stay by herself, but she didn't complain none. When

I'd come into her room in the mornin' early, she'd always say: ' Good mornin', Till,' jest as bright as could be. Right after she'd had her breakfast, she liked Miss Mary to run in an' talk to her for a while. After that, she liked to be by herself. Around three o'clock in the evenin' I went in to dress her. It was hard on her, and took her breath dreadful, but she wouldn't give in, an' she never got out of temper. When I'd got her dressed, Mr. Henry an' Sampson used to come up from the mill to lift her into her chair an' wheel her into the parlour. Mrs. Blake an' Mary would come in to have tea with her, an' right often Mr. Henry stayed for a cup. Missy was always in good spirits for tea, an' it seemed like her an' Mrs. Blake got more comfort out-a one another than ever before, talkin' about old times and the home folks in Loudoun County. An' Miss Mary was real fond of her grandma. If she'd knowed there'd been hard words ever, she'd forgot it. She had the right way with Miss Sapphy, an' it meant a heap, havin' her in the house that last winter; she was so full of life."

From the way Till spoke of Mrs. Blake's long visit, hints that she dropped unconsciously, one understood that there was always a certain formality between Mrs. Colbert and her daughter — a reserve on both sides. After tea, for the hour before supper, the Mistress preferred to be alone in the parlour. There were many snow-falls that winter, on into March. Mrs. Colbert liked to sit and watch the evening light fade over the white fields and the spruce trees across the creek. When Till came in with the lights, she would let her leave only four candles, and they must be set on the tea-table so placed that the candle-flames inside were repeated by flames out in the snow-covered lilac arbour. It looked like candles shining in a little playhouse, Till said, and there was the tea-table out there too, all set like for company. When Till peeped in at the door, she would find the Mistress looking out at this little scene; often she was smiling. Till really believed Miss Sapphy saw spirits out there, spirits of the young folks who used to come to Chestnut Hill.

And the Mistress died there, upright in her chair. When the miller came at supper-time and went into the parlour, he found her. The strong heart had been overcome at last. Though her bell was beside her, she had not rung it. There must have been some moments of pain or struggle, but she had preferred to be alone. Till thought it likely the " fine folks " were waiting outside for her in the arbour, and she went away with them.

" She oughtn't never to a' come out here," Till often said to me. " She wasn't raised that way.

Mrs. Matchem, down at the old place, never got over it that Miss Sapphy didn't buy in Chestnut Hill an' live like a lady, 'stead a' leavin' it to run down under the Bushwells, an' herself comin' out here where nobody was anybody much."

THE END

In this story I have called several of the characters by Frederick County surnames, but in no case have I used the name of a person whom I ever knew or saw. My father and mother, when they came home from Winchester or Capon Springs, often talked about acquaintances whom they had met. The names of those unknown persons sometimes had a lively fascination for me, merely as names: Mr. Haymaker, Mr. Bywaters, Mr. Householder, Mr. Tidball, Miss Snap. For some reason I found the name of Mr. Pertleball especially delightful, though I never saw the man who bore it, and to this day I don't know how to spell it.

WILLA CATHER

WILLA CATHER (1873–1947) was born near Winchester, Virginia. When she was ten, her family moved from the peace of Virginia to the wild prairies of Nebraska. She was graduated from the University of Nebraska at twenty-one, and did newspaper work and teaching in Pittsburgh, Pennsylvania, for the next few years. She published a book of verse, *April Twilights*, in 1903, and a book of short stories, *The Troll Garden*, in 1905. They were followed, over the years, by twelve novels, including *Death Comes for the Archbishop, A Lost Lady* and *Shadows on the Rock;* four volumes of short stories, and two volumes of essays. Willa Cather was awarded the Pulitzer Prize for fiction in 1923.

VINTAGE FICTION, POETRY, AND PLAYS

VINTAGE BELLES—LETTRES

2/03/01